Old friends against new friends . . .

"Hey, you guys! Guess what!" I called. Three angry faces turned to stare at me. Karen's eyes were still red from crying.

"How could you do that, Justine?" Roni demanded. "Chantale yelled at Karen, and you didn't even try to stop her."

I swallowed hard. "I'm sorry. I felt terrible, but I didn't know what to do."

"What to do?" Roni repeated. "How about be a good friend? You sure have a lot to learn about friendship, Justine. If you think those kids out there are your friends, then you need your head examined."

"Anyone would have been upset if they'd just had a new dress ruined," I said.

"That's ridiculous," Ginger said.

"It's okay," Karen said quietly, "Justine wants to fit in with her new friends. You shouldn't be hanging around in here with us, Justine."

"Yeah, Justine," Roni snapped. "You should get back to your *real* friends now."

Queen
Justine

#4

Queen
Justine

Janet Quin-Harkin

Rainbow Bridge
Troll Associates

To my dad, Frank Newcombe Lee.
I still miss him.

1

The Friday that changed my life started like any other day. It was one of those fall days in Phoenix when you finally have some hope that cooler weather is coming. The leaves were beginning to turn gold. School was boring enough to make me long for the weekend. I was really looking forward to Saturday night—we were sleeping over at Karen's for the first time, and her mother had promised to cook us Vietnamese food.

The girls at my old school probably would have laughed if they'd seen me getting excited about something as ordinary as eating Vietnamese food at somebody's house. They were the sort who would simply fly to Vietnam if they wanted Vietnamese food. Okay, so that's a slight exaggeration, but all the kids at Sagebrush Academy *had* been rich and used to doing really wild things.

I have a confession to make: I really didn't have such a great time at Sagebrush. I know I keep bragging about how great it was, but when I look back on it, I wasn't too happy there. I'd arrived in the seventh grade, and all the girls were already in tight little cliques. They were polite to me. They could even be almost friendly when they wanted to borrow something. But I always felt like an outsider there.

Come to think of it, I've always felt like an outsider everywhere, due to my father's habit of moving me from school to school whenever he got a better educational idea. He was away a lot on business, so he needed a school where I'd be looked after as well as educated. Or at least, that's what he said. I've lived with my father since I was three. That was when my mother walked out of our lives. I hear she's remarried with a new family now, but what do I care? I haven't seen her in so long that I don't even remember her. Who needs a mother, anyway?

My dad's remarried, too, and I do care about that! My stepmother makes Cinderella's look like Glinda the Good Witch. Get the picture? She's made all these new rules since she moved into our house, and she's bought lots of pastel furniture and freaks out if I spill something on it. She pretends she's trying to get to know me better when all she's doing is prying into my private life. There's more, but I don't want to bore you. Basically, I've made up my mind to hate her forever and ever!

. You probably think that my life isn't that great, and you'd be right if it weren't for Ginger, Roni, and Karen. For the first time, I've made some real friends. I mean, I've always had people who would come to my birthday parties and people to go skiing with. But I never felt like I had friends who really cared about me. Roni, Ginger, and Karen stuck with me through the first days at our new school, even though I know I was a snob then. That must mean they care about me, right? And I've had more fun with them at Alta Mesa High than I ever had at Sagebrush.

Frankly, I thought I'd die when my father announced he was putting me in a regular public school. He said now that he was married again, he wanted us to be a real family—a family that lived together full time and ate dinner together every night and all that stuff. I didn't want to be part of any family that included the wicked witch, but I didn't get a say in the matter. My first day of school was terrifying. Three thousand kids go to Alta Mesa and I didn't know a single one of them. I was sure that nobody would speak to me for four years.

Then I met Ginger, and she was nice to me. She introduced me to Roni, who introduced me to Karen, and we've been a foursome ever since.

So life at Alta Mesa was going pretty well so far, except for one rather major fact: I was the only one of the four of us who didn't have a boyfriend! I'm sure you're surprised—me, the best-looking, best-dressed one, and I'm the only one the boys don't seem to notice. How can that be? I bet if I was still at Sagebrush, I'd be dating a preppy jock from the guys' academy across the valley. The trouble is, there don't seem to be any preppy jocks at Alta Mesa. In fact, most of the guys we've met so far have been nerds . . . and I mean *nerds*.

We were sitting under our favorite tree at lunchtime that Friday when the nerd pack descended on us. These had to be the grossest guys in the universe, but for some reason, they seemed to think they were our friends. We were listening to Karen describe what her mother was planning to cook on Saturday, and suddenly we heard a familiar squeaky voice.

"Hi, ladies! Any big plans for the weekend?" It was Owen, the shrimpy nerd with the spiky hair, leader of the nerd pack.

Instinct made us gather up our backpacks for instant flight, but the nerds had us surrounded. They had this totally unnerving way of sneaking up on us silently. I don't know how they did it—maybe they came up through the soil. It would figure.

"Uh, yes, really big plans," Roni said. She's the quickest of us when it comes to thinking on her feet, and it was obvious that they were about to invite us to some horrible nerd-fest. "We have the most exciting weekend all planned, don't we, Justine?" she said, turning to me.

"We do? What?" I asked. Ginger dug me in the ribs, hard. "Oh, yeah," I said, nodding furiously. "Those plans. How could I forget something as exciting as that?"

In case you think I'm clueless, let me tell you that this sort of storytelling was not part of our routine at Sagebrush. We were instructed that honesty was the best policy and were brought up to be perfect ladies at all times. If we didn't want to accept an invitation, we'd just smile politely and say, "No, thank you, but we'd rather spend the weekend with a cockroach."

"Gee, that's too bad," Ronald said, peering at us through his heavy-rimmed glasses. He was the skinny nerd, very serious.

"Plans that can't be broken?" Wolfgang asked, his soulful brown eyes staring at us like a cow's. Wolfgang was almost as round as he was tall, and he wore the most disgusting sweaters—yes, sweaters, even in Phoenix. They usually had egg or ketchup spilled

13

down the front of them, too, which added to his complete lack of color coordination.

Last, and very much least, was Walter. He was the shy one, the computer whiz. At least, everyone always said he was the computer whiz, but when he'd tried to computer-match me with my perfect date, he couldn't come up with a single boy! This should give you some idea what the quality of guys is like at Alta Mesa. Maybe I'm just too picky.

Anyway, I'd rather throw myself off a cliff than go out with one of the nerds. Unfortunately, it didn't seem as if we could shake them off. The others had started feeling sorry for them, but not me! To me, the only good thing about the nerds was that they spent most of their time in a dark, spooky computer lab, away from the rest of the world.

"So what exciting things do you have planned, girls?" Owen persisted. He might be a shrimp, but he's not easily fooled.

"Well, let's see," Roni said, stalling for time.

"There's the dinner at my house, of course," Karen interrupted. "We'll spend all Saturday afternoon preparing it."

"That's right. The dinner," Ginger agreed.

"And of course there's the other big commitment we've got this weekend," Roni went on smoothly.

"Which is?" Owen insisted.

At that moment a group of non-nerdy guys came down the path from the gym. I recognized some of them from my classes. They weren't exactly the preppy jocks I would have preferred, but they were definitely better than what was currently surrounding us. Miraculously, one of the guys recognized me and started heading in our direction. His name was Danny Pandini and he was in my math class.

I'd had to change math classes because I hadn't covered a lot of the basics I needed for Algebra I/II. So now I was in Intro to Algebra, which took things more slowly. It was my only class without any of my friends. And it would have been terribly boring, except that Danny made it fun. He was always writing me notes or telling me jokes when the teacher wasn't looking.

His face lit up as he saw me now, and I thought what a very nice smile he had. His hair wasn't bad, either. A little too short, but dark and wavy. He had big, dark eyes that kind of crinkled at the sides. But he wasn't exactly what I'd call a snappy dresser.

"Hi, Justine. Hi, girls," he called, pushing his way into the circle of nerds. "Have you signed up to do your share yet?"

"Our share of what?" I asked.

"Pride Day on campus tomorrow," Danny said, giving me a friendly grin. "Don't tell me you haven't heard about it. There are flyers all over the place. We need a good turnout from the freshman class."

"What exactly is this Pride Day?" Owen asked suspiciously.

"The school can't afford custodians for maintenance work anymore," one of Danny's friends said, coming to stand beside Danny. "So we get volunteers to pick up litter, paint the trash cans, weed the flower beds, sweep up broken glass from the parking lots—you know, all the fun stuff."

I guess we didn't look too enthusiastic, because Danny went on, "It really is fun. I helped my big brother with it last year. They had a barbecue and we all got covered in paint."

He was mostly talking to me, and he seemed to want an answer. "Don't look at me," I said. "I hate getting messy. Just ask the others. I freak out if I get a spot on my clothes."

"She does," Karen agreed.

"But this is different. It's for a good cause," Danny pleaded. "I know it's easy for me. My old man's in garbage, so you might say that I'm in training to take over the business someday." He grinned.

I decided that I didn't think he was so cute after all. I mean, if my father was a garbage collector, I'd keep very quiet about it!

"So who can I sign up?" Danny said, producing a list on a clipboard.

Owen made a face. "Count me out," he said. "I don't touch garbage. I'm allergic to it. It makes me break out."

"I get hay fever from weeds," Ronald agreed.

"And I can't risk damaging my fingers," Walter added. "You need very delicate fingers to operate computer keyboards."

"I'm with them," Wolfgang chimed in.

"Pride Day!" Roni said loudly, making us all jump. "That was what we had planned for the weekend, remember? We already signed up. Aren't we on your list?" She grabbed the clipboard from Danny and studied it. "We must be on someone else's list, then. But we'll be there—you can count on us!"

She turned to the nerds. "Sorry you're not into garbage. We'll be up to our eyes in garbage all weekend, jumping in trash cans, scraping up chewing gum. You name it, we'll be doing it!"

"And having fun, too," Ginger added. I could see they were both trying hard not to laugh.

"Well, great," Danny said. "See you all bright and early tomorrow. Don't forget to wear old clothes. Bye, girls."

His group moved off to recruit more unsuspecting freshpersons. The nerds began to drift away, torn between their desire to spend the weekend with us and their dislike of garbage. I have to admit that I was torn, too. I wanted to be with my friends, but it was impossible that a day spent cleaning the campus could be fun.

"Justine, you are coming with us tomorrow, aren't you?" Karen asked.

"Are you guys really serious about this?" I said. "I thought it was just a way to get rid of the nerds."

Roni looked at Ginger and shrugged. "We told Danny we'd be there, so I guess we should show up."

"It might be kind of fun," Ginger added. "I bet Todd and Ben will have to be there. They make football players do stuff like that." Todd is Ginger's older brother. Ben is Todd's best friend and the current love of Ginger's life.

"That's right!" Roni exclaimed. "I know Drew's going to be there because he said something about a trash-filled weekend."

She was talking about the one and only Drew Howard, the current love of *her* life.

"I don't think I'll be able to get James to come and work," Karen said. You got it. James is the current love of her life. He's the only one I have a problem with. Ben and Drew are both cute. James is . . . well, James is cute, too, I suppose, but in a really weird way. He dresses like a cross between Batman and Zorro. I wouldn't be caught dead with a boyfriend who didn't know how to dress.

"But you'll come, won't you, Karen?" Roni asked her.

"Sure. If you guys are going, I won't desert you," Karen said. She turned to me. "So what about it, Justine?"

I took a deep breath. "Look, you guys, this just isn't me," I said. "I mean, I just had my nails done. And I don't even own any old clothes. I'm not sure where to buy them."

I stopped because the others were laughing. "What?" I demanded. "What did I say that's so funny?"

"Justine," Roni said, shaking her head. "You don't *buy* old clothes. Old clothes are . . . old clothes."

"But I don't have any," I explained. "When I get tired of something, I just throw it out. Why would you keep last season's clothes lying around?"

They were still smiling at me. I suppose I am funny to them, but I behave the only way I know how—the way everyone else did at Sagebrush. I know I'll have to learn to adjust to the real world, but it's going to take some time.

"Well, okay, if you really don't want to come," Ginger said, gathering up her bag and getting to her feet. "But you are going to be at Karen's tomorrow night, aren't you?"

"I wouldn't miss that for the world," I said.

2

You know how people can always tell you exactly what they were doing when a disaster struck? I mean, people remember the song that was playing on the radio when there was an earthquake—things like that. Well, I can tell you exactly what I was doing when my own personal disaster struck.

I had just arrived home from school and I was vegging out with a bowl of macadamia nut ice cream, watching a rerun of *The Beverly Hillbillies* and wondering why they didn't hire a wardrobe consultant with all that money. I was enjoying having the house to myself for once. My stepmother, the wicked witch, was out somewhere with my dad. I knew she was due back soon, because they were having guests over for dinner. So I was making the most of curling up in her new pink silk armchair and watching the giant-screen TV instead of the little set in my bedroom.

I had tried not to think about Pride Day on my way home. My friends had been sort of cold to me when we'd said good-bye outside the school gates. Maybe they thought I was letting them down by not taking part. But I really didn't want to spend my weekend picking up trash. I could understand why they were so eager to take part. If I had a cute boyfriend like Drew, it might have been fun to throw around paint with him. If I had a guy like Ben, we could have talked while we picked up trash. But I had nobody. I'd have to spend the entire day watching Roni and Ginger laughing and happy with their guys, while I was reminded that there was no special guy for me.

I thought about all this again as I sat curled in the witch's chair. I wasn't special to anyone in the world! I turned up the TV even louder. So loud, in fact, that I didn't hear the front door open.

The first hint I had that anybody had come in was the voice screeching behind me. "What is that awful noise? Justine, are you watching TV in the family room? You better not be eating in there."

Hastily I shoved my bowl of ice cream under the chair as the wicked witch walked in. I have to point out, in all fairness, that she doesn't look like a wicked witch. She is actually very beautiful—tall, slim, not a hair out of place, perfect makeup, great taste in clothes. She used to be a model, and she was the guest-relations expert at a big resort in Scottsdale until she married my dad. I can see why my father fell for her. She really was gorgeous. But just because she looks good doesn't mean she's any less of a witch. In fact, her pretty blue eyes were looking at me now with an icy glare.

"Turn that down, Justine," boomed my father's voice, right behind me.

I turned down the sound.

"Why do you have to have it so loud?" my stepmother demanded. "It can't be good for your ears to have it turned up that high. Two seconds of it was giving me a splitting headache!"

"And you do have your own set in your room," my father pointed out. "Why can't you watch TV up there?"

"Fine. Banish me to my room," I snapped. "I feel more like Cinderella every day. You'll have me scrubbing the floor and wearing rags next."

I started out of the room, but my stepmother touched my father's arm. "No, Jack, that's not right," she said. "Don't make her feel unwanted in her own house. Of course she's welcome to watch TV down here when we're not around."

23

"Yeah, right. When you're not around. That says it all," I snapped. "Everything's fine as long as I stay away from you."

"Justine, that's not fair," my stepmother began, but my father cut in.

"Justine, I won't have you being rude to Christine. She's trying very hard to get along with you. And she doesn't need any upsets in her life right now."

"It's okay, Jack," Christine said sweetly.

"No, it's not okay. I don't want you under any stress, understand?" he said to her. "In fact, shouldn't you be sitting down? Why don't you put your feet up, and I'll get you a cool drink?"

"Is Christine sick?" I demanded. She was acting all cutesy as she allowed my father to position her on the sofa.

"You're so sweet," she was giggling. "I'm perfectly okay, Jack, honestly. Women in China go on working in the fields until the ninth month."

I heard what she was saying, but my brain wouldn't accept it. It couldn't be possible. My father already had gray hair! He was . . . well, elderly. And she wasn't young, either. She spent a fortune on anti-wrinkle creams and spa treatments.

"Wait a minute," I interrupted their giggling. "Did I hear right? Are you saying that Christine's going to have a baby?"

Two excited faces looked up at me. "That's right, princess," my father said. "We just came back from the doctor's office and it's official. You're going to be a big sister. Isn't that wonderful?"

I stared at them as coldly as I dared. "Two old people like you? I think it's disgusting," I said. I ran across the marble entrance hall and up the stairs, two at a time. I could hear my father yelling to me and Christine saying, "Let her go, Jack. This has been a shock for her." But I didn't stop until I was safely in my room.

I closed the door and flung myself down on my bed, gathering my stuffed animals into my arms and burying my face in their soft fur. When Dad had announced that he was marrying Christine, I thought it was the very worst thing that could ever happen to me. For all those years we'd just had each other. Oh, I know he'd always been busy, but whenever he came to my school and took me out for the day, he tried his hardest to give me a good time. He took me to expensive stores and let me buy whatever I wanted. He let me bring my friends to the best restaurants. He always called me his princess.

But now he had a new princess, someone he liked better than me. And he would definitely like his new child better than me. I could picture how it was going to be: Everybody fussing over a dumb baby,

25

and the kid allowed to touch all my old toys and mess up my room, and nobody giving two hoots if I was alive or not.

And it was embarrassing! How was I going to tell anyone at school that I was about to become a big sister? Everyone else's brothers and sisters were already playing Little League!

I lay there for a long time, hugging Teddy Blue and Panda and Hump-free Bogart, my camel, breathing in their familiar smell and feeling the fake fur tickle my face. I needed someone to hug me back, someone who was alive and cared about me. Suddenly I realized something: I had friends now. I could call up Roni and Ginger and Karen and they'd care. They'd know how to make me feel better.

I reached across to my bedside table and picked up the phone. I called Karen first. I was sure she'd understand. After all, she was an only child, too. She could imagine what a shock it would be to have a baby brother or sister.

The phone rang several times. Then a voice said hesitantly, "Hello. Who is this, please?"

I remembered Karen had told me that her mother hated answering the phone.

"Hi, Mrs. Nguyen, it's Justine," I said. "Is Karen there?"

"Oh, Justine, hello," she said, her voice softening.

"Sorry. Karen is not here. She's with James. You know James? The boy with the long hair? She's at his house. They work at computers together. Don't ask me. I don't understand what they do, but Karen likes it. Then they're going to a movie."

"Oh," I said. "Will you ask her to call me if she doesn't get home too late?"

"Very well. I'll tell her," Mrs. Nguyen said. "Goodbye, Justine." Then she hung up.

I fought back my disappointment that Karen wasn't around when I needed her. That dumb James was taking up all her time now. I dialed Roni's number.

"Please be there. Please answer," I prayed. Her voice came on the line. "Roni?" I almost yelled. "It's Justine."

"Oh, hi, Justine. What's up?"

"Guess what," I began, "I just found out that my stepmother's going to have a baby—"

"No kidding? That's great, Justine. I'm so happy for you. You'll have so much fun taking care of a little baby! I bet it adores you and follows you everywhere." She didn't give me time to say anything. "I remember how sweet Paco was when he was just born. He'd smile at me and I'd feel so proud! I'm glad you called to tell me, but I've got to go. Drew's playing football at Tempe tonight. I have to go cheer him on. See you tomorrow, Justine."

Then she hung up, leaving me feeling like a deflated balloon. How could she think I'd be happy with something like a baby? I mean, I like babies in theory, but not in my house and not when the baby is going to take my place!

I was about to call Ginger when I remembered that if Roni was going to watch Drew play football, then Ginger would be going to watch Ben. She wouldn't have time for me, either. It really was true: I had nobody who cared about me.

A little later, there was a tap on my bedroom door. My father came in and sat on the end of my bed.

"I realize this must come as a shock to you, princess," he said. "It's a bit of a shock for us. We're delighted—thrilled—of course, but it's been a long time since I had to change diapers, and Christine . . . well, Christine hasn't had much to do with babies."

"No kidding," I said, thinking of Christine's long, polished fingernails. I wondered how she would handle the baby throwing food on the furniture.

"So I want you to try extra hard to be nice to Christine," he went on. "It's not going to be easy for her, adjusting to this new role. She needs support and understanding. I'm counting on you, Justine."

I wanted to ask him who was going to support *me*, but the words wouldn't come out. I was scared that

I'd cry if I said anything. So I nodded and looked away.

"That's my girl." My father leaned across and gave me a quick peck on my forehead as he got up. "The Franklins are coming to dinner tonight. He's very big in securities trading," he said. "So I thought that maybe you'd like to spend the evening over at a friend's house?"

"All my friends are doing something except me," I said.

"Well, why don't you join them?" he asked brightly. "I'll run you over . . ."

"No thanks. I'd only be in the way," I said. "Besides, I don't like football."

"Then maybe you need to find friends with interests more in tune with yours," he said. He always said things like this, as if making friends was the easiest thing in the world. Didn't he realize how hard it was to find anyone nice in the first place? Now he wanted me to change my friends the way I'd change outfits.

"There aren't too many people at Alta Mesa who are into ballet and fencing and all the stuff we did at Sagebrush," I said. "It's football or nothing."

He chuckled as if this were funny. "You'll find your niche, princess," he said. "A school with three thousand students has to have some of our kind of people. There are plenty of upscale families who send their kids to public school, especially a school with the reputation of Alta Mesa. This Ted Franklin sends his kid there, and he's worth millions. I'll talk to him about it tonight and see if he's got any suggestions."

"It's okay. I can handle my own life," I said.

"But I want you to be happy, princess."

I wanted to say, "Then send Christine away," but I knew that would only make him explode again. So I just shrugged and started arranging my stuffed animals on my bed.

3

Friday night I lay in bed thinking of how mad I was at my friends for deserting me and listening to the conversation floating up from my father's dinner party.

That Mr. Franklin sure had the loudest voice. I bet he didn't even need a telephone to do his securities trading with the New York stock exchange!

"You wait until Little League, Craft," I heard him booming. "Then you'll find out what it really means to be a father. Hours and hours sitting on a hard bench, watching kids swing and miss. That's true fatherly dedication for you."

"We don't even know if it will be a boy yet," Christine said with her silly laugh. "Although I know Jack is dying for a son."

"You bet I am," my father said. "And I'm kind of looking forward to Little League and Pop Warner and all that stuff. It will be a new experience for me. I missed all that with Justine."

"Well, girls are different," Mr. Franklin's voice boomed on. "I can't say that I ever wanted to go to Chantale's dancing lessons. I leave that sort of stuff to Mrs. Franklin, don't I, sweetie?"

Chantale, I thought. I'd heard that name mentioned around school. Someone had pointed her out to me once, but she wasn't in any of my classes. I'd have to ask my friends about her when I slept over at Karen's. Unless, of course, they'd decided to cancel the sleepover in favor of romantic evenings with Drew, Ben, and James!

Boys created all the problems in life, I decided. It even seemed as if my dad was disappointed that I wasn't a boy. I turned over and put the pillow over my head. Now I had one more thing to worry about. It had never occurred to me that my father had always wanted a son, or that he was hoping for a boy now. I could picture him and his darling son, doing stuff together, lost in their own little world. He'd never been that way with me.

My dad had always been awkward around me. He'd taken me places and crammed in lots of activities. I'd thought this was because he wanted to give me the best time possible. But now it dawned on me that he wanted to keep me busy—so that he wouldn't have to spend time talking to me or getting to know me.

A tear squeezed itself out of the corner of my eye. I wondered if they'd send me to another boarding school when the baby came. That way, I wouldn't be around to distract them from their son. Or maybe they'd want to keep me here as an unpaid baby sitter.

It took me a long time to fall asleep. Even with my head under the pillow and my door closed, Mr. Franklin's laugh echoed through my skull. I finally drifted off after I heard the front door slam.

I woke to find the sun streaming in on me. It was almost eleven—too late to think about showing up at Pride Day, even if I'd wanted to.

"Okay," I told myself, "I'm not going to sit around brooding and feeling sorry for myself. I'm going to have a fun day, doing all the things I like."

I was in the middle of fixing myself strawberry waffles with bacon when Christine came into the kitchen. Her face turned an interesting shade of green.

"What are you cooking?" she demanded.

"Just waffles and bacon. You have a problem with that?"

"Oh, no, that's fine. Just wipe the stove when

33

you're done," she said. Then she hurried out of the room.

So this was the famous morning sickness. It wasn't just something you saw in old movies. It really did exist—and Christine had it! I found myself grinning as I thought of all the interesting recipes I could try out in the next few months. *I know how to get back at you, wicked witch,* I thought. But even as I imagined this, I realized that the sicker Christine became, the more my father would fuss over her, and the more he would ignore me. I couldn't win either way.

I didn't even enjoy the bacon and waffles. I tipped half of it into the garbage and headed out for the mall. Luckily, there was one within walking distance.

I love malls. Malls are the one place where I feel right at home. That upbeat background music and the fountains and palm trees and the smell of pizza and coffee calms me right down. As soon as I step inside a mall, I feel like I've escaped to an enchanted place where my problems are far away. I hoped that was how I'd feel today.

I walked all the way down one side of the upper gallery and back up the other. I tried on five different sweaters, seven pairs of jeans, and a prom dress (just in case somebody asked me to the homecoming dance, which was only a couple of weeks away). But I didn't buy anything, which is unusual for me. I never leave a mall empty-handed. I just wasn't in a shopping mood that day. The last few times I'd been here, I'd been with Karen, Roni, and Ginger. It had been fun to try on things and then critique one another's outfits.

I came to the sad conclusion that shopping by myself wasn't fun anymore. I didn't want to make a decision on a prom dress until I had Roni or Karen with me. Especially Karen. She had such warm, friendly eyes. I liked the way her whole face lit up when she was excited about something. I always knew she meant it when she told me something looked good on me.

I sighed. They were probably having fun at that dumb Pride Day. I could just see Roni and Drew having a paint fight, or a garbage fight—Roni would do anything!

I headed for the food court, although I wasn't really hungry. I wanted to be in a place where I didn't feel so alone. I was eating under a big palm tree when the piped music started playing "When a Man Loves a Woman."

I can't help it. That song just does something to me! I closed my eyes, letting the music throb through me. When I opened them again, I found myself staring at this incredible guy who was dressed, head to toe, in black leather. He had long dark hair and a face that looked as if it was chiseled out of fine granite. A rugged, strong, independent face—the kind you see on commercials for men's cologne. He was staring into space in a bored sort of way.

Suddenly he must have realized I was looking at him. His dark eyes held mine until I blushed. He winked at me. Then he turned and walked away with catlike grace. A group of kids was waiting for him by the entrance. The girls gazed up at him adoringly as he approached, but he acted kind of cool, as if he didn't care what they thought of him. I was pretty sure that he didn't wink at any of them!

I finished my drink hastily and wandered toward the entrance, not taking my eyes off that sleek, leather-clad guy for a second. If he smiled or winked at me again as I passed, that would mean he liked me—right? But before I got that far, the group of kids headed for the exit, pushing through the swing doors and scattering incoming people as if they owned the place. They were just passing through the door when a guy's voice yelled, "Yo, Stryker, wait up!"

The leather guy glanced over his shoulder and waited for his friend. I suddenly experienced a major dose of déjà vu. I'd seen this happen before at school. It was a miracle! I actually knew this guy! I remembered seeing him with this same group out in the Alta

Mesa parking lot. I'd thought then that there was something wild and dangerous about him. I'd been too far away to take a good look at his face, but it had to be the same person. After all, there couldn't be too many guys in the world named Stryker, could there?

"Stryker," I whispered. What a neat name. It suited him. Justine and Stryker—not bad. It was much better than boring old Ben or James. *Oh, are you going out with James tonight, Karen? I'm going with Stryker on his bike. . . .* I could picture it clearly. It didn't matter that he had been surrounded by girls and he didn't know me. Fate had brought us together today. Of all the girls in the mall, I was the one he had winked at. That must mean he thought I was special.

I pushed my way out into the sunshine just as four motorcycles roared past. Stryker was leading them. His hair streamed out from under his helmet. I thought he looked like a creature from another world . . . like a god. I knew at that moment that I had to meet him, or die.

4

I couldn't wait to get together with my friends that night. I had so much to tell them, I thought I'd burst. Besides, I now had a job for the Boyfriend Club! All the way home from the mall, I thought about how I could possibly meet Stryker. And suddenly it hit me: The Boyfriend Club could arrange it!

I suppose I'd better explain about the Boyfriend Club. It had started out as a joke when we were sleeping over at Ginger's house one Saturday night. We were pretty desperate to meet boys at our big new school. So we decided that what we needed was a club that matched us up with the guys of our dreams. We'd laughed about it to begin with, but the more we talked about it, the better it sounded. I mean, if we saw a guy we thought was a mega-babe, we'd probably be too shy to go up and introduce ourselves to him. But the Boyfriend Club would find out all about him for us, track his habits, and find out what he liked. They could even plan a situation in which we could "accidentally" meet him.

Sounds like a great idea, right? We all thought so. Of course we soon discovered that things don't always go according to plan. In fact, none of our plans had worked out the way we thought they would. True, Ginger, Roni, and Karen now all had boyfriends, but that wasn't exactly thanks to the Boyfriend Club. But now, at last, the club had a chance to show that it really could work. All my friends had to do was snoop around for me and find out everything there was to know about Stryker. I was so excited that I sat on the edge of my seat as my dad drove me over to Karen's house.

"You look more cheerful than you did last night, I must say," he commented, nodding with satisfaction. "I know the news about the baby gave you a jolt. But now you're looking forward to it as much as we are, I can tell."

"Something like that," I said. I didn't tell him that if everything went according to plan, I'd be out of there on the back of a motorbike, heading for the hills, when the dumb baby was born.

It will serve them right, I thought. *I'll make them wish they'd paid more attention to me.*

There were good smells coming from Karen's kitchen as she opened the door.

"Hi, Justine. We were wondering where you were," she said. "We missed you today. In fact, I called your house around lunchtime to tell you we were having a great time. We wanted you to come join us, but your stepmother said you'd gone out somewhere."

"Yeah," I said. "I went to the mall."

Karen led the way into her kitchen, where Roni and Ginger were concentrating on wrapping food into little bundles.

"We're making cha gio, Justine," Ginger said, looking up as I came in.

"Excuse me?"

"Vietnamese egg rolls. They're called cha gio," Ginger explained. "It's not as easy as it looks. The shrimp keep jumping out."

"I told you they were fresh," Roni quipped. "Get your jacket off and come help us, Justine. We'll get a production line going here. I'll cut up the wrapper, Ginger will put in the shrimp and vegetables, you'll moisten the edges, and Karen will roll them up."

I couldn't believe it. They were acting like this was any ordinary day, like nothing had changed in

41

the universe, when my whole life had taken a turn for the better. I took my place without saying another word.

After a while, I noticed that they were looking at me suspiciously. I guess I'm not normally so quiet.

"So where did you go today, Justine?" Ginger asked. "We tried calling you to come with us."

"Yeah, Justine, you should have come," Roni said. "I don't think I've ever laughed so much."

"There was this group of girls," Ginger said, grinning broadly. "They were some sort of snobby club called the Kestrels, and they all showed up in matching aprons and rubber gloves to pick up the trash."

My friends seemed to think this was funny. But I certainly would have wanted to wear an apron and rubber gloves if I'd been expected to pick up chewing gum from the sidewalks!

"Apparently your family had to be on the Mayflower to be invited to join this club," Ginger continued. "Even you've never acted as snobby as they did, Justine. They didn't seem to notice that ordinary people exist."

"And you know Danny, that friend of yours?" Roni interrupted. "You should have seen his impersonation of them! We nearly died. He's so funny. Over lunch he was telling us all these weird stories about things his dad found in the garbage! One woman thought she'd thrown her diamond ring into the garbage by mistake and she insisted on going through the whole truck!"

I shuddered and decided I was glad I hadn't been there. I wasn't really into garbage stories.

"Yeah, Justine, he was a blast!" Karen added. "He did this whole Las Vegas routine with a broom. Everyone was cracking up."

"Look, he's not my friend, okay?" I said. "He just happens to be in one of my classes. I hardly know him."

"Okay, keep your hair on," Roni said. "What we're trying to say is we had fun and we missed you."

I shrugged. "I had more important things to do."

"She was at the mall. Can you believe it?" Karen said. "What a waste of a sunny Saturday."

Roni smiled. "Oh, of course, how dumb of me. I forgot about the baby. I bet you went to all the baby stores with your stepmom," she said.

"I did what?" I couldn't hide the disgust in my voice.

Roni looked surprised. "What's up?" she asked.

"You don't know me very well if you think I'd want to spend any time with my stepmother, especially now!" I growled. "And if you think I'd be excited about some stupid baby . . ."

"You mean you're *not* excited about being a big

sister?" Karen asked. "We thought you would be. You loved playing with Roni's little brother. You told her how lucky she was."

"That was different," I said. "Just because babies can be cute doesn't mean I want one in my house."

"I'd love to have a little baby brother or sister to take care of," Karen said wistfully.

"Not if your parents didn't want you around in the first place," I snapped. I moistened my wrapper and dumped it in front of Karen.

"Oh, come on, Justine. It can't be as bad as that," Ginger began.

I shook my head furiously. "It's worse," I said. "The wicked witch never wanted me around. From the moment she moved in, she's made me feel like I don't belong. And when the baby comes, I know exactly what it's going to be like. All their attention will go to the baby. It will be like I don't exist. My father's already talking about Little League. He never did any of that stuff with me." I bit my lip and turned away, pretending to be busy with my egg roll.

Roni put her arm around my shoulders. "I'm sure it won't be like that, Justine. When the kid grows up, you'll be the one he adores. I love it when my little brother climbs on my knee and asks me to read him a story. It makes me feel very special."

I shook my head. "I bet they'll send me to another

boarding school when the baby comes," I said. "They'll probably need my room for the baby."

"No way, Justine. They can't send you away again. We won't let them," Karen said fiercely. "I'll go tell them myself that you have to stay put."

"That's right," Ginger added. "It's not good to move someone during their high school years."

"Besides, you're becoming a normal person for the first time in your life. Moving would ruin all our hard work," Roni joked.

I looked from one face to the next. My friends wanted me to stay! They were prepared to fight for me. I felt a tear trickle down my cheek. "Thanks, guys," I said, hastily wiping it away. "I was thinking that nobody cared about me, but I guess I was wrong. I was really depressed today when I went to the mall."

"You went all by yourself?" Karen asked. "No wonder you're depressed. Malls are awful when you go alone. It's like everyone else is having a good time but you."

"As it happened," I said, "I did have a good time. I met the most incredible guy!"

"You did?" Karen asked. "What was he like?"

"Gorgeous. Drop-dead cute. Long black hair, rugged sort of face, dressed head to toe in black leather—kind of a Johnny Depp look-alike."

"And you met him? He talked to you, out of all the girls at the mall? Get real, Justine," Roni said, grinning.

"Am I so disgusting that no cute guy is ever going to look at me?" I said.

"Of course not, but . . ."

I could see by their faces that they didn't believe me. They didn't think that I'd ever meet a guy like that. They probably thought I was making it up because I hadn't been having fun with them at Pride Day. And I did tend to talk big sometimes, when I wanted to make an impression.

"You don't have to believe it if you don't want to," I said. "But I'm telling you, he was the most gorgeous guy I've ever seen and he did notice me."

"For real, Justine?" Ginger asked. "What did he say?"

I meant to tell them the truth, but it sounded so lame. Okay, so I hadn't actually met him. Our entire contact had been one wink. I heard myself saying, "I was sitting at a table, minding my own business, when I felt him looking at me. You know how you get the feeling someone is staring at you? I looked up and there he was, totally cool. And when he saw me looking at him, he gave me this sexy smile and winked at me, and he said, 'Hi, babe. All alone?'"

They were sure paying attention to me now. "And then what?" Roni demanded.

"He came over and he put one foot on the chair beside me and he said, 'Haven't I seen you somewhere before?'"

I didn't even realize I was lying anymore. I could actually hear his voice in my head. "And you know, he did look familiar," I continued, "but I wasn't sure where I'd seen him. And then he said, 'I'm Stryker. Who are you?'"

"And then?" Karen asked excitedly.

"And then his friends started yelling for him to hurry up and he said, 'Gotta go. See you around.' He left before I could tell him my name."

They were all staring at me. I could tell they were impressed. I was pretty impressed myself. "And guess what?" I went on, enjoying the spotlight. "I realized as he walked away that I *did* know him. I'd seen him in the parking lot at school, with a whole lot of guys on motorbikes. I followed him down to the entrance and I watched him ride away. He was so gorgeous."

"He doesn't sound like your type, Justine," Roni said cautiously. "I would have pictured you with a country-club preppy guy who drives a BMW."

"So would I, until now," I said. "But this guy is different. I get the feeling he's dangerous and exciting. And I need some excitement in my life right now. I just have to find a way to meet him again."

"How are you going to do that?" Karen asked.

"I thought that's what the Boyfriend Club was for," I said. "You guys are supposed to help me get together with him."

"I don't know about bikers, Justine," Karen said with a nervous laugh.

"It's only a question of research," I said. "You ask around. You find out where he hangs out, and you arrange for us to meet. It's as simple as that."

"Right," Ginger said, laughing. "Simple as that."

"Justine!" Karen wailed. "You've stuck the wrong edges together. All the stuff's fallen out of the cha gio."

"Sorry," I said, picking shrimp off the counter. "I guess my mind's on other things today. It's like in twenty-four hours I've gone from being totally depressed to being totally excited. I just can't concentrate on minor things like egg roll wrappers."

"Those minor things are our dinner tonight," Roni said, "and I for one am starving. It was hard work painting all those garbage cans."

"And painting Drew," Ginger added.

"That's right," Roni said, starting to giggle. "At least the garbage cans stood still and let me paint them. Drew kept dodging away."

"You were very mean to him," Karen said.

"He got her back," Ginger said quickly. "Didn't you see when she was cleaning up in the girls' bathroom and Drew managed to get a hose in through the window?"

"He missed me," Roni said. "It was a good idea, though."

They were all laughing so hard that—for a moment—I actually wished I'd been there. I tried to imagine what it would be like if Stryker had been chasing me around with the hose.

"Danny asked where you were," Karen said with a knowing look. "He said, 'Where's your friend with the cute blond ponytail?' He looked disappointed when he heard that you hadn't shown up."

"What's with this Danny stuff?" I asked, wrinkling my nose. "You guys should know me well enough by now. I mean, do I look like someone who'd want to go out with a garbage collector's kid?"

"He can't help what his father does for a living, Justine," Ginger said. "My dad drives heavy equipment. Does that make me a bad person?"

"And mine landscapes people's yards," Karen said. "Are you only going to talk to Roni because her dad's the one with a white-collar job?"

"I didn't mean it like that," I said. "It's just that . . . well, garbage is different. I mean, garbage is gross! And anyway, I am not interested in Danny."

"Okay, we get the message," Roni said.

"If you guys really are my friends," I said, "then

you've got to help me with Stryker. He's the guy I want. I'm counting on the Boyfriend Club to make it happen."

"We'll do our best, Justine," Karen said, "if you're really sure that Stryker isn't just a fantasy for you."

"I'm really sure," I said. "And I know he wants to meet me again."

Even as I said it, I felt my cheeks getting hot. What if I met him again and he didn't even remember who I was? But that wink had been special, hadn't it? You didn't go around winking at just any girl. . . .

"Are the cha gio all ready to cook, Karen?" Mrs. Nguyen asked, coming into the kitchen. She looked at the messy counter and the sloppy rolls we had made.

"Sort of," Karen said.

"Holy Toledo! You girls are like a tornado in my kitchen," she said, but she didn't look angry. It sounded so funny to hear someone saying "Holy Toledo" in a Vietnamese accent that we all started giggling. Mrs. Nguyen shook her head and began to herd us away like sheep. "Go on, move out of the way so I can get the dinner cooked."

She pushed us aside and started dropping the rolls one by one into hot oil, using a pair of chopsticks. Soon we sat down to spicy chicken, sticky rice, the egg rolls, some little dishes with salads, and dipping sauces. It was delicious, and we ate way too much.

Later that night we lay in sleeping bags in Karen's room and she played her violin for us. It was sweet and soothing and romantic. As I lay there with closed eyes, I began to imagine that anything was possible. I was going to meet Stryker again and he'd invite me for a ride on his bike. I didn't know how or where I was going to meet him, but I knew that somehow, I had to make it happen.

5

I got to school early on Monday morning and hung out on the front steps of the administration building. I was determined to watch Stryker arrive. I told my friends I'd see them in class, and I waited until the first bell rang. I even waited until the second bell rang, and then I had to sprint to class at the last minute.

All through health ed, our first class, I thought about Stryker. I wondered if I'd gotten it wrong after all. Maybe it wasn't him I'd seen in the parking lot that day at school. I nudged the girl sitting in front of me.

"Hey, Cindy, do you know a guy called Stryker?" I whispered.

"No, why?"

"Just wondering."

I went back to my work. Cindy was a cheerleader. She was the type who knew everybody. If she didn't know Stryker, that was a bad sign.

After morning classes ended, I told my friends to go to lunch ahead of me, and I headed for the parking lot. Some cycles were parked against the fence. One of them looked like the one Stryker had been riding. I walked up to it. It was big and powerful, gleaming with chrome. I ran my hand over the smooth leather seat, imagining myself sitting there, my arms tightly around Stryker's waist. . . .

I must have been almost in a trance, because I was jerked awake by the screech of brakes. I looked up. A group of kids was crossing the street, all dressed in black leather. Both boys and girls had long hair, and they looked pretty menacing as they walked across the street together, not caring about the traffic. Cars screeched to a halt and the kids kept on walking as if they hadn't even seen them. It was like they owned the street. I was impressed. As they came closer I saw Stryker. He was at the back of the group and he moved with that wonderful animal grace.

Suddenly I realized that I had no reason to be hanging around their bikes. I'd feel like a fool if they saw me, and I wanted Stryker to be impressed the

54

first time we truly met. I dodged away between the parked cars. I was creeping back to the buildings at a half-crouch when a cheerful voice called out, "Hey, Justine, are you playing spy? Can I play, too?"

I looked up. There, at the head of the row of cars, was Danny, grinning at me. Now I really did feel like a fool. What possible explanation could I give for sneaking between cars all hunched over like that? My mind went totally blank. I was about to do what I always do when I'm caught off guard—shoot my mouth off. I wanted to say that I was studying the quality of garbage dropped in the parking lot—a subject I knew he could appreciate—but something stopped me. I could almost hear Roni's voice in my head, asking me what mean thing Danny had ever done to me. He didn't deserve a put-down when he was just being friendly.

"I, uh, lost an earring. I was looking for it," I said, glad that some reasonable excuse had come to me.

Instantly he was walking toward me. "I'll help you look. They don't call me Hawkeye for nothing." He pulled a macho pose, and I couldn't help smiling.

"So what does it look like?" he asked. He put his hand up to my head and turned it sideways. Then he said, "Justine, you're already wearing two earrings. Don't tell me you have another ear hidden somewhere."

"I lost it last week," I said. "The earring, I mean,

55

not my other ear. It could be anywhere. It was just a little gold stud. I guess it's hopeless, really, but thanks for offering to help."

"Any time." Danny leaned against a car. "We missed you on Saturday. It really was fun."

"So I heard," I said.

Suddenly there was a burst of loud music. Stryker and his friends were passing us on their way to afternoon class. I turned back hastily, hoping that they wouldn't notice me talking to Danny. I didn't want Stryker to think that I hung out with guys who wore plaid flannel shirts and had short, neat haircuts.

"I'm going to give up on the earring, thanks," I said. "I don't know why I was wasting my time. I've got a zillion more pairs at home."

"Was that pair your favorite?" Danny asked. "I know I get really attached to things. I've got a favorite pair of socks. One day the washing machine swallowed one of them, and I took the whole darned thing apart just to find it. So I know how you feel."

I tried not to look at him, but I was thinking, *This is a guy who develops relationships with socks. What am I doing talking to him at all?* I wanted to get out of there as quickly as possible, back to my friends and sanity.

"I have to run," I said. "I promised my friends I'd meet them. See ya, Danny."

"See ya, Justine," he said, giving me a big, hopeful smile.

Roni, Karen, and Ginger were waiting for me under the big tree where we always ate lunch. Let me tell you that nobody in Phoenix eats outside between April and November. It's just too hot. But we'd tried the cafeteria a couple of times and found it totally unbearable—noisy and crowded. Besides, all the tables were always taken, except the nerd table. After the dining room at Sagebrush, it was real culture shock for me. So I was glad the others preferred the tree outside. At least we had our privacy there, and it was pretty cool in the shade.

"There you are," Roni called. "We were worried about you. Where have you been?"

"Just doing my Stryker research," I said.

I saw them exchange nervous glances. Karen cleared her throat. "Look, Justine, we don't think this is a good idea at all," she said. "We understand that this guy is very cute and exciting and all, but we think he might be a little too exciting for you."

"What she means," Ginger interrupted, "is that we've been doing some research of our own, and Stryker sounds really wild."

"He plays drums in a rock band . . ." Karen began.

A rock band? Hey, this was sounding better and better. "So?" I demanded. "Would you turn down a

57

chance to go out with Eddie Vedder if you could?"

"It's just you're not that kind of girl, Justine," Roni said kindly. "Those rock groupies—the sort of girls who hang around Stryker—they know how to take care of themselves. They're tough."

"Ben says Stryker hangs out with a really rough group," Ginger said. "He thinks they're probably into drugs."

"Just because someone wears black leather and plays in a rock group doesn't necessarily mean he's into drugs," I said. "Anyway, I'd like to be able to judge for myself. I'm not stupid, you know. I'd like to get to know the guy better and then decide."

"Okay," Ginger said cautiously.

"So, have you guys found out where he plays with this rock band? That sounds like a good way to meet him."

Ginger glanced at Roni. "I don't think we should be telling you this."

"Oh, come on," I said impatiently. "This is what the Boyfriend Club is supposed to do—arrange meetings, not make moral judgments about who's suitable and who's not. And I'll only find out for myself if you don't tell me."

"Okay, he plays in a club called Blackwater Fever on Saturday nights," Ginger said.

"Blackwater Fever?" I asked. "Where's that? I've got to go there."

"I'm pretty sure this club is in a bad part of town," Roni said with a worried frown. "I've heard people talking about it. It's one of those clubs over by the interstate."

"So? Lots of trendy restaurants are in bad parts of town. It's what makes them trendy," I said carelessly.

"But this is different, Justine," Roni said. "This is the sort of place you see on the news—the sort of place the police raid. I'm sure we wouldn't be allowed to go there, even if we wanted to."

"And I bet they don't let in people our age," Karen added. "Don't you have to be twenty-one to get into clubs?"

"Then how do Stryker and his friends get in? They can't be twenty-one yet."

"I bet they have fake IDs," Ginger said.

"So we'll get them, too." I unwrapped my sandwich. "I'm sure it's easy if you know how. We'll just borrow somebody's."

Ginger laughed uneasily. "Justine, get real," she said. "Nobody's going to believe we're twenty-one even if we could borrow an ID, which I'm sure we can't. So let's drop this whole crazy idea, please."

"You mean you won't come with me?" I asked, looking from one face to the next.

"We're not going and neither are you," Ginger said firmly.

"Yeah, Justine," Roni added. "This whole thing is getting out of hand. We're your friends. We care about you. You led a sheltered life up there at Sagebrush Academy. This Stryker guy is not for you! If you want a rock star, get a picture of Eddie Vedder, put it on your wall, and drool over it. But forget the real thing, because it's going to lead nowhere but trouble."

Karen put her hand on my arm. "Justine, we just want what's best for you. And Stryker's not it, I know it."

"You don't know it," I said, my cheeks flushing angrily. "You hated it when I tried to tell you that James wasn't right for you, and now you're trying to talk me out of meeting the one guy I've been interested in since I got here." Karen tried to interrupt, but I held up my hand and went right on talking.

"All I want to do is meet him, have a chance to talk to him, then I'll make up my own mind. I'm very grown up for my age. It's not like I've never been out of Arizona. I've traveled around the world, you know. I've had to handle bullfighters in Spain and mountain climbers in Austria. . . ."

I saw them glance at one another.

"Justine, shut up," they said in unison.

They always tried to shut me up when I talked big. It annoyed the heck out of me. For one thing, I hated

60

knowing that all my bragging hadn't fooled them one bit. I glared at them. "Fine, if you don't believe me," I said. "But you can ask my dad—"

"Justine, we don't care about Austria," Ginger interrupted. "We just don't want to see you doing something totally dumb."

Karen touched my arm again. "Promise us that you won't try and go to this Blackwater place," she said.

"Yeah, Justine, promise us," Roni said. "Because if we find out you're going to do anything as dumb as that, we'll have to tell your folks."

I was horrified. "You wouldn't snitch on me! Some friends you are."

"It's because we *are* your friends," Roni said. "We think you've flipped out, and we're going to stop you any way we know how."

"Okay, I get the message," I said quietly. "I guess you guys know best. I'll forget all about Blackwater Fever and watching Stryker play his drums."

They smiled at one another and at me.

This time I did have them fooled.

Now that I knew what my friends thought about Stryker and Blackwater Fever, I realized that I'd have to proceed with great caution. I had to see Stryker playing at the club, whatever they thought. But I was too afraid to go there alone.

So I came up with a great, foolproof plan: I'd invite my friends to sleep over at my house on Saturday night. I waited until the subject came up on Thursday, as we were all leaving school together.

"So, who's coming with me to the game on Saturday?" Roni asked.

"I promised Ben I'd go watch his JV game," Ginger said, "and they're playing over in Glendale, so I can't be two places at once."

"And I already told James I'd help him with his computer," Karen said.

"Which leaves you, Justine," Roni said, turning big, dark, imploring eyes on me. "You don't have anything to do, do you? You know how I hate going anywhere alone."

"But Roni, you know I don't like football," I said. "It really upsets me to see all those nice uniforms get so dirty."

They all laughed again, as if I'd said something funny, but it's not funny to me. I was brought up to keep my clothes looking perfect. I've never in my life wanted to roll around in the mud.

"Please, Justine," Roni said. "Pretty please with sugar on top?"

She made such a pathetic face that I had to laugh. "Oh, okay. I guess I don't have much choice, do I?" I said. "I'll suffer through a football game for the sake of letting you drool over Drew for a couple of hours."

"Justine, you're all right, you know that?" Roni said, slapping me hard on the back. "And who knows," she added with a grin, "maybe you'll find the love of your life at the game. Maybe some cute guy will come up to you and tell you that he's noticed you around school but has been too shy to speak to you before."

"Yeah, right," I said. "He'll probably be wearing a muddy uniform and smell bad." I was careful not to say anything about Stryker. For them, the subject was closed.

"But after the game I want you guys to sleep over at my place," I said.

"I thought we were going to Roni's," Karen said. "We were going to make tamales."

"We can make tamales some other time," I said, talking very fast. "I really want you to come to my house instead. My folks are going out to a party, and they won't be back until two or three."

"So, all the more reason to sleep over at Roni's," Ginger said. "That way it won't matter what time your folks come in, because you won't be there."

"But they like me there to keep an eye on the house," I insisted. I know it was a pretty lame excuse, but it was the only thing I could think of. To tell you the truth, I'd forgotten about Roni and the tamales. "There have been so many burglaries in the neighborhood, and you know all the valuable stuff we have. . . ."

"They want you to guard the house?" Roni said, grinning at the others. "Justine, you freak out when we watch horror movies. You hid behind the couch last time. Can you see yourself defending the house against burglars? You'd probably run screaming out the back door."

"So? That would scare the burglars away," I said. "My screams are pretty impressive, you know."

"We know," Ginger said. "We heard them when we were watching the horror movies."

Karen touched my arm. "I get the feeling it's pretty important to you that we sleep over at your place," she said gently. "I'm sure we can make tamales at Roni's some other time."

"Sure," Roni said. "I just didn't think you'd care that much if burglars carried off your stepmother's furniture."

"She doesn't," Karen said, giving me a sweet, knowing smile. "I think she wants to let her folks know that it's her house, too. She belongs there with her friends. We know how insecure she's feeling about the new baby."

I swallowed hard. Roni and Ginger obviously

accepted Karen's explanation. I felt like a heel for not telling them the truth, but I just had to have them with me on Saturday night. I just had to get to Blackwater Fever and watch Stryker!

Chapter

6

On Saturday I went to the football game with Roni, like I'd promised. I wasn't looking forward to it, I can tell you. All that mud and brutality is so gross. I guess I must be anti-violence at heart, as well as anti-mess. But I knew that I needed Roni as an ally tonight, so I wanted her to owe me a favor.

After the game I went home to get the house ready for the sleepover. Christine was trying extra hard to practice her mothering skills.

"Do we have enough snacks and sodas to keep you guys happy all evening? And what about movies? Do you want to go down to the video store with your father and pick out some? Are you going to want to make popcorn?"

I found all this motherly fussing totally nauseating. She'd hardly noticed I was alive before. Well, she wasn't going to fool me with her newfound sweetness. Christine had started off as my enemy and she was going to stay my enemy. She was probably only being nice to me because she wanted me to be her unpaid baby sitter for the next ten years. But I had to smile when she said, "Now, do you have enough to keep yourselves occupied all evening?"

If you only knew, I thought.

She fussed over me until she and my dad left for their party. "Are you sure you're feeling up to it, honey?" I heard him ask her as they headed for the door. "We don't have to go if you think it will be too much for you. . . ."

I held my breath, waiting for her answer. *Feel up to it,* I commanded silently. Two parents in the house sure would spoil my plans.

"Oh, don't worry, Jack. I'll be fine," Christine said. I let out my breath in a huge sigh of relief. She had been looking kind of pale and weak lately. Even all that makeup couldn't always hide the fascinating shade of green her face became when she looked at food. I kept hoping my dad would stop paying so much attention to her now that she didn't look gorgeous anymore. But it never seemed to bother him.

My friends arrived around eight. "So where are we

going to sleep?" Roni asked. "Outside in the cabana by the pool might be fun."

"Too many bugs," Ginger said. "I vote for Justine's room. It's so pretty. I'm not used to sleeping in a bedroom where everything matches."

"Are we allowed in the living room to watch the big-screen TV, Justine?" Roni asked, bouncing around the house excitedly. "I love MTV on the big screen with the volume turned way up!"

I took a deep breath. "Actually, guys, I've got a different plan for us tonight," I said.

"You have? What?" Three excited faces looked at me.

"I thought we might pay a visit to a dance club."

"Dance club?" At first they looked confused, but it gradually dawned on them what I was saying. "Justine, you can't be serious!" Karen exclaimed. "You're not thinking of going to that Blackwater Fever place, are you?"

"Why do you think I wanted us to be over here tonight?" I said, grinning excitedly. "My house isn't too far away. We can take a taxi—"

"No, Justine, absolutely not," Ginger said. "We are not going anywhere near that place."

"Then I'll go by myself," I said bravely.

"No, you won't," Roni said. "I thought we talked you out of all this craziness. We're not letting you go to any club. We'll lock you in your room if we have to."

"I'd climb out the window," I said.

"Then we'll sit on you all night!" Roni insisted. "We'll tie you to the bedpost. We'll shut you in the laundry closet. We'll do whatever it takes to stop you!"

"You can't stop me," I said. "I've made up my mind. I want to go more than anything in the world, and if you won't come with me, I'll go alone. But I thought you were my friends. I hoped you'd come with me."

Karen put her hands on my shoulders. "Justine, just listen to yourself," she said. "You've totally freaked out. Let's get a grip on reality here. You don't belong at a wild club. You don't belong with a guy called Stryker. Face it, you really don't have much chance of getting this guy interested in a cute little freshman like you. This is just some weird fantasy."

"Okay," I admitted. "It *is* a fantasy, I guess. But I have the biggest crush on this guy. I just have to watch him play his drums tonight. Please come with me. We'll go by taxi, and we'll just take a peek. We don't even need to go inside—we'll peek in through the door. Then we'll come right back before it's too late, I promise. What can possibly go wrong?"

They were looking at one another uneasily now.

"Please," I begged. "Please come with me. I'm

really scared to go alone, but I want to go so much. Maybe Stryker will never notice me, but it means so much to me to see him again. I'm really serious about this. I'm going tonight, and I'm going alone if I have to."

"I guess we don't have much choice," Roni said at last. "We're your friends, and we can't let you go alone to a place like that. But we're only going to take a peek, like you promised. We are definitely *not* hanging out there."

"I promise," I said. "Just a peek, that's all I need."

"Then I guess we could go around nine o'clock," Ginger said, looking at Roni for approval. "Nothing would start too early at a place like that. Are you going to phone for a taxi, Justine?"

"You bet," I said, "but first I have to go change. Come with me. Let's choose an outfit that will make Stryker notice me."

After half an hour of going through my closet we had to admit that I had no biker gear. Everything I owned made me look like a little freshman. Karen wanted me to stick to jeans and a white shirt, but I decided on the only leather clothing I owned: a black miniskirt with my highest heels.

"We want to look old enough so they don't get suspicious," I said, generously applying my darkest lipstick.

"We're not going to look old enough, whatever we

do." Karen shook her head. "I really have a bad feeling about this, Justine. I wish you wouldn't go through with it."

"What's so terrible about it?" I said. "We'll arrive in a taxi. We'll tell the taxi to wait. We'll tell the person at the door that we just want to take a peek, to see if a friend is there. We'll watch Stryker for a couple of minutes, then we'll come right home. Simple."

"I hope so," Karen said softly.

"I don't know why you're making such a big thing of this," I said. "It's not as if I'm asking you to rob a bank for me. I went with Roni to watch a dumb football game and that was way more dangerous. We nearly got run over by a pack of muddy guys."

My friends had to laugh at this.

"Justine, you're something else," Roni said.

"If I get to watch Stryker tonight, I'll be a happy something else," I said, beaming at them. "Come on, let's go call the taxi."

A little while later, we were speeding through the darkened streets in the cab. I knew my friends were nervous, especially after we left my elegant, tree-lined neighborhood and headed into a part of town we'd never seen before. We passed a couple of sleazy motels and a freeway underpass where some weird-looking guys were hanging out. It was raining, which it hardly ever did in Phoenix. I stared out through the dripping windshield and fought with my fear. I had really believed that I could handle a bad part of town. Now I wasn't so sure.

"Here you are, ladies," the taxi driver said. "Are you sure this is what you want?"

I wasn't sure that this was what I wanted at all, but I handed the driver a ten-dollar bill. I tried to tell him to wait for us, but my voice was drowned out by the loud music blaring from the club. The driver just nodded and, to our horror, drove away very fast.

"I thought you were going to ask him to wait," Karen said shakily.

"He didn't hear me."

"How are we going to get back?" Roni asked. Her voice sounded shaky, too.

"There must be a phone. We'll call for another cab." I sounded much braver than I felt.

As we walked toward the club door, we could see two large shapes outside. I'd never seen a bouncer before, but I recognized them right away. They were stopping a group of kids from going in.

"Let's see your ID," I heard one of them growl.

Karen grabbed my arm. "I knew you had to be twenty-one to get into clubs like this! We don't have IDs."

The kids at the door turned away and walked, muttering and cursing, back to their car.

"I told you we should have borrowed my sister's ID," I heard one of them say. She looked a lot older than us. I swallowed hard.

"Maybe they'll just let me peek inside if I say I'm looking for a friend," I suggested.

"Good luck," Roni said, glancing across at the two walking mountains in the doorway.

"There has to be a back door," I said.

I headed around the building, hoping that my friends were close behind me. Sure enough, there was another door at the back. Before I could chicken out, I opened it and stepped inside. There was a great blast of sound. I could feel the vibrations of the drums going right up from the soles of my feet and through my body. There was light at the end of the passageway. I crept along until I found myself standing just behind the stage. I peeked through the back curtain. Strobe lights were flashing, musicians were playing, and dark shapes were dancing in the shadows below.

It took me a while to see that the drummer wasn't Stryker. It was a guy with stringy blond hair and a mean-looking face. Stryker was nowhere around. I'd come all this way and Stryker wasn't even there!

Fighting back tears of frustration, I went back along the hallway. I'd almost reached the door when two shapes appeared out of nowhere. Two girls in

74

leather jackets stood between me and the door. I thought I recognized them from the parking lot at school.

"Hey, where do you think you're going?" one of them said, glaring at me.

"I was just checking to see if a friend of mine was here," I said. "But he's not, so I guess I'll be going. . . ." I tried to edge past them to the door, but one of the girls grabbed my arm.

"Okay, who put you up to this?" the other girl demanded.

They had scratchy voices and their faces looked hard and mean. My heart was hammering. "Up to what?"

"Oh, come on, Little Miss Innocent," the girl sneered. "I saw you hanging around our bikes in the school yard, and now you show up here. Who sent you?"

"Wh-what do you mean? What do I have to do with you?" My life was passing before my eyes. I was sure something terrible was going to happen.

"I don't know. You tell us," the second girl said.

"You've got it all wrong," I said, looking frantically for Roni or Ginger. "I came to meet a friend, but he's not here. I'm just leaving, okay?"

"Okay, then get out and stay out," the bigger girl said. She only gave me a little push, but I wasn't expecting it. It sent me staggering out through the door so suddenly that I fell into the nearest puddle. My friends came running over.

"Justine, are you okay?" Roni cried, dragging me to my feet. "You had to be off your rocker, going in there. What happened?"

"I met two of Stryker's friends," I said, attempting to brush the mud off my leather skirt. "They weren't very friendly."

"And Stryker?"

"He wasn't even there."

"You mean we came all this way for nothing?" Ginger asked.

"I'm sorry. I was so sure . . ." I swallowed hard, determined not to cry in front of my friends. "I'll call another taxi and we'll go home and have some hot chocolate, okay?"

But it wasn't that easy. There was no phone outside the club, and they wouldn't let me in. We started walking, looking for a gas station with a pay phone. The rain was coming down in cold, drenching sheets, bouncing off the sidewalk and stinging our faces.

I felt terrible, and not just because the rain was ruining my leather skirt. I had put my friends through the worst night in history, and they weren't even complaining. I had been totally crazy to go through with this, and they had come with me even though they knew it was

76

the dumbest idea since Custer decided to make a stand.

"At least it can't get any worse," I said, trying to sound cheerful. That was when my high heel got stuck in a crack in the sidewalk. I tried to wrench it out, but all I succeeded in wrenching was my ankle. I felt a hot, shooting pain in my leg, and the heel came off my shoe. My friends tried to support me, but I could only walk forward at a slow hobble.

"There must be a gas station somewhere," I said, peering through the driving rain.

"Maybe this is all just some cosmic joke," Roni said, but none of us laughed. We were too ready to believe it.

Just then a motorcycle sped past, spraying a sheet of water all over us. The guy riding it looked a lot like Stryker.

We were soaked and shivering by the time we finally found a phone. It was another half hour before the taxi got there. Nothing had ever looked better than the lights shining from my house as we pulled up outside.

"Hot showers, hot chocolate, and dry clothes for everyone," I said. "Doesn't it feel great to be home and safe?"

But my relief was a little premature. As I pushed open the front door, I heard my father's voice. "Justine? Where the devil have you been?"

Chapter
7

I tried to think of a reasonable explanation, but none would come. My mind was a cold, dripping blank. All I could say was, "Dad! You're home early."

"Christine wasn't feeling well," he said. "We came back to find all the lights on, the girls' belongings all over the floor, and no sign of you. Needless to say, Christine completely went to pieces. We've been on the phone with the police for the past hour. I've just sent her off to bed to rest. Do you have any idea how bad it is for her to go through something like this?" He was glaring at me accusingly.

"I'm sorry, Daddy," I muttered, staring at my muddy feet. "We didn't mean for it to happen."

"And just where have you been?" he demanded.

"You look like a pack of drowned rats."

"We just went to a club to see a friend," I muttered, "but the taxi didn't wait for us. We had to walk home most of the way in the rain. I hurt my ankle."

I was hoping to drum up some sympathy, but I wasn't getting any. He was still scowling.

"You know you're not allowed out at night without permission," he said. "And you must know that you wouldn't be allowed at any club! I suppose you all had this whole thing planned?"

He glared at each of my friends in turn, as if he was trying to decide who was the ringleader.

"Don't look at them," I said. "It was my idea. They tried to stop me. They only came with me because they were worried about me."

"And with good cause, it seems," he said. "You'd better get your friends upstairs and into dry clothes, while I call the police to tell them you're safely home. And go apologize to Christine!"

At any other time, I'd have told him that there was no way I was apologizing to Christine, but I heard myself saying, "Okay, Daddy." What else was there to do? I led my friends up the stairs, hobbling painfully on my twisted ankle. None of them said anything, not even Roni. They went into my room and started changing out of their wet things. I went to talk to the wicked witch.

Christine was lying in the darkness as I opened her door. She sat up right away and flicked on the bedside light. "Justine!" she cried, "Oh, thank God you're safe."

I looked at her in amazement. Her face was all swollen and blotchy, and her eyes were red. She'd been crying.

"I'm sorry I made you worry," I muttered.

"I just couldn't imagine what had happened to you," she said. "You've never been out this late without telling us where you were. I thought something dreadful must have . . ." Her voice trailed off as she got her first good look at my appearance. "What on earth happened to you?" she gasped. "You look terrible!"

It figured. For a second there it actually sounded as if she cared about me. It was almost like I imagined a mother would be. But then came the typical put-down—*Oh, you look terrible, Justine.* Any minute now she'd complain that I was dripping water on her white carpet.

"Yeah, I don't feel too great either," I muttered. "We had to walk back in the rain and I twisted my ankle."

"Where did you go?" she asked.

"I went to see a friend, okay?" I said sullenly. "You're always telling me I don't make friends, but when I go watch a friend play drums at a rock club, I get in trouble."

81

"Well, you didn't ask permission first," she said.

"You wouldn't have let me go if I'd asked," I said, eyeing her accusingly. "The moment you heard the words *rock club* you'd have freaked out. You still treat me like a child."

"Justine, that's not fair. We let you do all the things other kids do," she said. "But I can't imagine what kind of parents would let their fourteen-year-olds go to a rock club. Did Roni and Karen and Ginger go along with this harebrained idea? Or was it their idea in the first place? I always thought that Roni was a little wild for you."

"Just leave my friends out of this, okay!" I shouted. "It was my idea and nothing happened and we're back home. So calm down! Now, if you'll excuse me, I need to take a shower before I catch pneumonia and you lose a free baby sitter."

Then I made my grand exit, slamming her door behind me. My friends were waiting in my room, huddled together, looking miserable.

"Okay, showers first," I said, "then hot chocolate. Follow me."

"Justine, what about your ankle? It looks enormous," Karen said. "Didn't your stepmother think you should see a doctor?"

"She didn't even notice it," I said. "She was too busy telling me that I have the wrong kind of friends."

"Wow," Ginger said. "She really is a witch. Come on, Justine. We have to get you some ice for your ankle."

I let them help me into bed and put an ice pack on my ankle.

"I don't care what my stepmother says," I said. "I've got the best friends in the world."

"Yeah, well, you'd better remember that the next time you ignore our excellent advice," Roni said with a grin. "I don't ever want to go through that again!"

"Me neither," Karen and Ginger said in unison.

Luckily my ankle healed itself pretty quickly. I wrapped it up in an Ace bandage and was walking around on it the next day. My friends went home kind of early. They had been very quiet all night. I think the adventure had shaken all of us. I apologized over and over again for what I'd put them through. They were really nice about it, but they still wanted to get to their own homes. I couldn't blame them.

Dad and Christine didn't say anything to me all day. But when we were sitting down at dinner that night, Dad suddenly turned to me and said, "After what happened last night, Christine is worried about you, Justine."

"It's okay." I shrugged. "You don't have to worry. I'll never try a stunt like that again."

"We know that," he said. "We think you've learned your lesson. But it does highlight an important fact about you: You're finding it hard to make the right kind of friends at your new school."

"I've got great friends." I frowned. "Roni, Ginger, and Karen are the nicest girls you could ever find."

"I'm sure they are," my father said, glancing at Christine for support. "It's just that . . . well, they're also newcomers to Alta Mesa. They don't know anyone else, either. You're used to being in the middle of things, princess. Think of all the dances and parties and ski trips they arranged at Sagebrush."

"It's true, Justine," Christine put in. "I think that you're a little bored now. You have too much time on your hands, and it's made you look in the wrong direction for excitement."

"That's not true," I began. But then I stopped, wondering. Hadn't I been interested in Stryker because I was looking for something exciting? Shocking my folks had something to do with it, but excitement was definitely a big reason, too.

Christine smiled encouragingly. "Your father and I talked about it, and we realized that what happened last night was partly our fault. We put you into a big public school and expected you to sink or swim. Of course you had trouble making friends—the people you mixed with at Sagebrush had all been carefully screened. How could you know how to meet the right friends?"

"I'm not exactly stupid, you know," I said.

"The point is," my father interrupted, waving his finger in that I'm-about-to-give-a-lecture style, "that it's about time we helped you meet the right sort of people, Justine. *Our* sort of people. There are several members of the country club who send their kids to your school. We'll arrange for you to meet them."

"I can make my own friends, Daddy," I said, fighting to be polite.

"Obviously you can't, if last night is any indication," he began, but Christine touched his arm.

"Of course you can make your own friends," she said quietly, "but it can't hurt to get into the social swing of things, can it? The holidays are coming up and it would be nice to be invited to the right sort of parties and dances, and to meet the right sort of boys."

I hated to admit it, but she did have a point. There couldn't be any harm in being invited to parties and dances—and it would be fun, too.

"Your father has been on the phone to his friend Ted Franklin," Christine went on. "His daughter goes to your school, and she's very active socially."

"Chantale? I hear she's a snob," I said.

"I'm sure she's a lot of fun when you get to know her," Christine replied. "And she's certainly very popular."

"Then I'm sure she wouldn't be interested in getting to know a little freshman like me," I said.

"On the contrary," my father said, looking pleased with himself. "As I say, I was on the phone to the Franklins today. Chantale will try to get in touch with you at school tomorrow. It seems she belongs to a little club that you might want to join."

The Kestrels, I thought. That had to be it—those girls my friends had laughed at on Pride Day, the ones with the matching aprons. Was that what I wanted for my high school future?

"You have to start somewhere, Justine," Christine said.

Again, I had to admit she was right. Everybody I knew so far I had met through Roni, Ginger, and Karen. I had no circle of friends of my own. And now that the other three all had boyfriends, they were spending time with their boyfriends' friends. I was being left out.

Besides, I thought. *It might make sense to meet some of the kids who belong to the country club. Maybe I could meet a boy there—one who's more my type than Stryker.*

"I'll give it a try, I guess," I said.

My father came around the table and gave my shoulder a clumsy pat. "That's my girl," he said. "I know you and Chantale are going to get on just famously."

8

"So how did it go with your dad and stepmother?" Karen asked me. "Are they still mad at you?"

We were standing under our tree at lunch on Monday—the ground was still too wet to sit on. This was the first opportunity we'd really had to talk since Saturday night.

"They were pretty nice about it, actually," I said. "I expected to be grounded forever, but they said that they understood how hard it is to make friends at a new school. They thought that was why I'd been chasing after the wrong type of kids."

"Gee, thanks a lot," Roni said. "You make it sound like we're pond scum."

"They didn't mean you," I said hastily. "And I told

them that you were the best friends anyone could ever have. But they still think that I need to get involved in more activities. Actually, I think they're right. I don't really do much besides eat and go shopping. It's not like Sagebrush, which was one big social whirl."

"Well, pardon us for not being one big social whirl," Roni said, grinning at Ginger.

"I didn't mean it like that," I said. "You have no idea what it was like at Sagebrush. There was always something going on—ski weekends, dances, ballet performances, concerts. . . . We never had a chance to be bored."

"I guess life must seem pretty tame to you after that," Karen said softly.

"But I like doing things with you guys a lot more than I liked the activities at Sagebrush," I told her. "The girls there were all so snobby and spoiled. I never had fun like we have when we're together. Still, I suppose I do need to develop some interests here. If only they had a ballet club, or a fencing club. I'd be one of the hot shots!"

I saw my friends grinning at one another.

"You could always start a ballet club with the nerds," Roni said. "Remember how Ronald was just dying to dance *Swan Lake*?"

"Oh, please," I said, making gagging noises. "If I

have to join a club that includes the nerds, then I really am in big trouble! Actually, my father wants me to meet a group of his friends' kids. I don't know if they'll want to hang out with a little freshman nobody like me, though. I bet they won't even look for me."

Almost on cue, we glanced up to see a girl coming down the path toward us. She was dressed in a tartan kilt and a white shirt, about the preppiest outfit I'd seen since I came to Alta Mesa. She paused when she saw us, wrinkled her forehead as if she was deciding whether we were okay to talk to, then started across the grass toward us.

"Is one of you Justine?" she asked.

"I am."

I saw her size me up—the way I was dressed, my hair, my makeup. Evidently I looked okay, because she handed me a small white envelope. "Chantale wanted me to give you this," she said. "Chantale Franklin. Your fathers know each other."

"Thanks," I said, taking the envelope.

"Open it right away or you'll be late," the girl said, scurrying off.

The others were looking at me with interest. "What was that all about?" Ginger asked.

"It's what I was just telling you about," I said.

"Chantale Franklin is the person my father wants me to meet."

"You'd better open your letter," Roni said. "It sounded pretty important."

I slit it open. The envelope was lined with gold and there was a gold border around the little note inside. At the top was a picture of a bird. Underneath, in gold letters, it said, "The Kestrels request your presence at . . ."

Under that was written in ordinary pen, "their weekly business meeting in room 242, Monday, at 12:30 sharp." The word *sharp* was underlined. It was signed "Chantale Franklin, President."

"Is it an invitation to something?" Roni asked, peering over my shoulder. "Pretty fancy note-paper."

"It's to a business meeting of the Kestrels," I said.

"A what? Are you serious?" Ginger sputtered. They all started laughing.

"They send you a gold-leafed note just to ask you to a meeting of their dumb club?" Roni cried. "I don't believe it."

"Are they for real?" Ginger agreed.

"Why do they want you to come to their meeting anyway?" Karen asked.

"I suppose they might want to invite me to join their club."

"Justine! You're not going to go, are you? Weren't they the weirdos who wore matching aprons at Pride Day?" Roni looked disgusted.

"I guess I'll have to go, since my father set this whole thing up," I said, "but I don't have to join if I don't want to."

"I should hope not," Karen said. "You should have seen those girls on Pride Day. They acted like a bunch of snobs, Justine."

"And we've just trained you out of all that Sagebrush nonsense," Roni said. "We don't want you slipping back again."

"Don't worry about me," I said. "I hate snobby people as much as you do. Save me a cookie from your dessert, Karen—I'll be back in a little while."

I got up and headed into the school. Once I was out of sight of my friends, I checked my jeans for dirt and ran a quick brush through my hair. If these Kestrels were anything like my old friends at Sagebrush, appearance mattered a lot to them.

"Why am I getting nervous about this?" I asked myself. "Why should it matter to me what a bunch of snobs think?" But it did matter. I didn't want them to think I was an unimportant nobody. I took a deep breath and fluffed my hair again before I knocked on the door of room 242. Someone called "Enter," and I opened the door.

It was just an ordinary classroom, with girls sitting at most of the desks. I don't know what I'd expected—some kind of exclusive, tastefully decorated lounge, I guess. Chantale was sitting at the teacher's desk, along with two other girls, both very preppy looking. In fact, a quick glance at everyone in the room gave me a major case of déjà vu—I felt like I was right back at Sagebrush Academy.

"Justine!" Chantale said, beaming at me as if I was her long-lost sister. "Welcome to the Kestrels. I'm so happy to have found you at last. My father mentioned that you'd come to our school, but I hadn't been able to locate you."

I felt like saying that I'd eaten lunch under the same tree every day since school started, but I didn't think that would get us off to a good start. I just smiled sweetly and said, "Thanks for inviting me to your meeting."

Chantale turned to the rest of the group. "Justine has just arrived here from Sagebrush Academy. Her parents belong to the same country club as my folks, and they wanted me to make her feel welcome and get her involved in things."

Obviously, I was now acceptable in their eyes. They were all looking in my direction.

"Sagebrush?" one of them said. "Do you know Alison Westover?"

94

"My parents almost sent me to Sagebrush! How was it?" asked another.

"Isn't it a shock going to a public school after a private one? I freaked out when I came here from St. Clare's," confided the girl sitting nearest the door.

"Do you belong to the Junior Golf section at the club?"

"I've seen you playing tennis there, haven't I?"

It seemed I was suddenly everyone's friend. Everybody in that room had some connection with me—same country club, friends who went to Sagebrush, parents who did business with my dad or lived in our neighborhood. I was amazed how many ties I had with all these people I'd never met before. I felt like an orphan rediscovering my long-lost family.

In spite of telling myself that I wasn't interested in joining the Kestrels, I had to admit it felt good to be back among people who spoke my language. They were all talking with me as though we were best friends, until Chantale rapped her gavel on the table.

"Kestrels, we are in the middle of an official business meeting," she reminded us. "You're all out of order. There will be time for socializing later. Please take a seat, Justine. You are item five on the agenda.

We're still only on item three: the dance. Molly, would you give your report on how the preparations are going?"

A slim girl with dark brown hair and a preppy mini-kilt got to her feet. "Number of tickets already sold: sixty-five. I expect that number to rise to about ninety, based on last year's attendance. Hardly any of the boys have RSVP'd yet."

"Typical," someone muttered. "I bet they all make up their minds at the last minute."

"They'll have to let us know by this weekend," Chantale said, "because I have to finalize things with the caterer by then. Now we'd better go over the details of the golf tournament, since it's coming up on Saturday. Serena?"

"We've got eleven teams so far," Serena said, "although it would be so much easier to schedule with twelve. But if Justine is going to join us . . ." She looked at Chantale for approval.

Chantale turned to me. "We're talking about our upcoming father-daughter golf tournament at the country club this Saturday," she explained. "Of course you're not officially a Kestrel yet, but do you think you'd be interested in attending?"

I had played golf before—everybody who lived anywhere near the resort town of Scottsdale played golf. But I had only played twice in my life, and both times were complete disasters. Still, the words *father-daughter* were echoing through my head. My dad had wanted me to join this club, hadn't he? He couldn't refuse my first Kestrel function. A picture came into my mind: Me and my dad, together in a golf cart all day, laughing and joking as we rode around the course, while Christine stayed home, looking pale and green. "I'd love to," I said.

"Great." Chantale nodded her approval before turning to the rest of the group. "I think we should skip to item five and talk about Justine before we finalize the golf tournament. It seems difficult to leave her hanging like this."

"I motion that we move to item five and discuss Justine," one of the girls said.

"I second that motion."

I wanted to laugh. Fifteen girls sitting alone in a classroom, and they were acting like the U.S. Congress. But nobody else was smiling.

"Justine comes to us highly recommended," Chantale announced. "She has connections with most of us Kestrels already, and it seems like she'd be a natural addition to our club. Would somebody like to officially nominate her for membership?"

A pale-faced girl next to Chantale rose to her feet.

"I nominate Justine Craft for membership in the Kestrels," she said.

"I second her," came a voice from the floor.

"All those in favor of accepting Justine, raise your hands," Chantale said. I think every hand went up. The only strange thing about all this was that nobody had asked me if I wanted to join. I wasn't even sure what I was joining.

"Congratulations, Justine," Chantale said, coming over to shake my hand. "It's a great honor to be accepted into the Kestrels as a freshman, you know. Some people wait for years to be invited. I know you'll be a credit to our club and uphold all our traditions."

"I don't really know anything about the Kestrels, or what traditions I'm supposed to be upholding," I mumbled.

"Of course you don't," Chantale said. "We're a secret organization. We make a vow that nothing said in this room is ever repeated to an outsider."

"But what exactly do the Kestrels do?" I asked.

"We divide our time between charitable work and social activities," she said. "We've got the golf tournament—the entry fees go toward our Thanksgiving baskets for the poor—and the following Saturday is our annual fall dance at the country club. The profits from that will also go to our baskets for needy families. It's one of our little traditions. It's all explained in our Kestrel motto. Shall we show Justine, Kestrels?"

The girls all rose to their feet and started chanting:

"Kestrels spread their wings,
Kestrels soar to the sky,
Kestrels look down on the whole world
And see what they can do to make it a better place."

As they recited their motto, the girls all spread out their arms as if they were flying. I thought they looked pretty stupid, but I forced myself to keep a straight face. At least the part about looking down on the whole world was accurate!

I could just imagine Roni's face when I described it to her . . . until I remembered that if I became a Kestrel, I'd be sworn to secrecy. That meant I couldn't even tell my best friends what went on here—unless, of course, they joined the Kestrels, too!

For a second I was excited about the idea. Then I remembered how Roni, Ginger, and Karen had laughed at the Kestrels. They would never want to hang out with girls who wore aprons. Anyway, these girls were all daughters of families that belonged to the country club. Obviously my friends wouldn't be the sort of people the Kestrels were looking for.

I was torn. The father-daughter golf tournament and the dance sounded great—I'd actually get to meet some boys from the private schools in the area. But would it be any fun without my friends? And did I want to join a club so snobby it would turn down people like Karen, Ginger, and Roni? On the other hand, my friends didn't want anything to do with Chantale and the Kestrels, either. Maybe *they* were the ones being snobby.

I didn't have time for any more debate with myself, because Chantale stood up and beckoned to me. She had a Bible in her hand, just like they do in court.

"Okay, Justine, raise your right hand," she said. "Do you swear that you will uphold the principles and traditions of the Kestrels? Do you vow to make this world a better place and preserve beauty wherever you go? Do you promise that you will never reveal what goes on at our secret meetings?"

I wasn't sure what to do. Chantale looked at me. "Say 'I promise,'" she whispered.

"I promise," I muttered. There didn't seem to be much choice.

"Justine, you have promised to keep our sacred oaths. I now pronounce you a member of the Kestrels,"

Chantale said. Everyone broke into applause.

Now Dad will be happy for me, I thought. It didn't seem to matter whether I was happy about the Kestrels, as long as he was proud of me. My friends would understand that, right?

9

My friends were waiting for me on the steps outside the building. They were grinning as I came out.

"So how did the meeting go? Was it funny? Tell us everything," Roni said, linking her arm through mine as she propelled me across the quad.

"I can't tell you too much. I'm sworn to secrecy," I said.

"Sworn to secrecy! What do they do—compare how much money their fathers make?"

"It was a very ordinary business meeting," I said, "but for some reason, they have a code of secrecy. I had to take a vow of silence."

They all burst out laughing. "Justine, it's like joining an order of nuns!" Karen said. "You didn't go for all that stuff, did you? They didn't brainwash you into joining?"

"I, uh . . ."

"You *did* join?" Roni glared at me in horror. "Justine, how could you? We finally had your snob disease cured."

"Well, I didn't have much choice," I muttered. "They didn't ask me if I wanted to join. They just shoved a Bible in my hand and made me swear."

"Swear what?"

"I can't tell you," I said. "But look, guys. I had to go through with it. My father had it all arranged—he would have been mad if he'd heard that I turned Chantale down. I want him to be proud of me. I don't have to stick with the club if I don't like it."

"Are you kidding?" Karen said. "Try getting out of it and they'll probably set their Labrador retrievers on you."

"They'll whip her with their rubber gloves!" Roni giggled.

"They'll smother her to death with their aprons," Ginger said.

"You're being silly," I said, laughing nervously. "It's just an ordinary service club and they do some pretty neat things. At least I'll have a social life now when you guys are all out with your boyfriends. I've already signed up for the father-daughter golf tournament on Saturday."

"Father-daughter golf!" For some reason my

friends seemed to think this was hysterical.

"I suppose golf was on the curriculum at Sagebrush, along with the ballet and the fencing," Roni said, digging Karen in the ribs. She put on a fake snobby accent. "It's a terribly social game, you know."

They were all giggling now. I quickly changed the subject. "And next weekend they have a dance coming up. They've invited boys from all the private schools. It's really formal, so I get to buy a new prom dress and wear a corsage . . . all that stuff."

"If that's the kind of thing that makes you happy, then I guess it's great," Karen said.

"Karen!" Ginger exclaimed. "Who could actually be looking forward to a father-daughter golf tournament? And to weekly meetings with the Kestrels?" She wrinkled her nose in disgust.

Karen looked at me with understanding. "Well, it makes sense for Justine. Her family belongs to a country club, and her dad plays golf. I'm sure all the Kestrels are just like her. Maybe it will be fun."

"At least my dad will have to spend some time with me now," I said. "He's got no choice, since he got me into the Kestrels in the first place."

"So how did it go at school today?" Christine asked me as we sat down to dinner. "Did Chantale get in touch with you?"

"Better than that," I said. "I'm now a member of her club! It's called the Kestrels. They all belong to the country club and they do all the kinds of things you'd approve of."

"Well, that's just wonderful," Christine said, turning to my dad for approval. "It seems like Justine has found her niche at last, thanks to your little talk with Mr. Franklin."

My father beamed at me. "That's great, princess. Glad to help."

"What are some of the things they have planned?" Christine asked me, sounding really interested.

"There's a father-daughter golf tournament on Saturday," I said, delighted that the first event was one that didn't include her.

"This Saturday?" my father asked, wrinkling his forehead. "Gee, that's too bad. I have a meeting at eleven."

I shot him a horrified glance. "But Daddy, you have to come," I pleaded. "We're officially entered. All the Kestrels are going to be there. I can't be the only person who doesn't show up for my first official Kestrel function. You wanted this for me. You arranged it!"

"She's right, Jack," Christine said. "We can't let her be the only one who doesn't take part in her first social function. Couldn't you postpone your meeting?"

"I suppose I could ask Johnson to meet me on Monday instead," my father said slowly. "You're right. It's up to us to get Justine started in the right social direction. Okay, I'll do it. Better brush up on your golf swing, princess. What's your handicap?"

"My what?"

"Your golf handicap."

"Uh, I'm not sure." This was awful. What if I was so terrible, he wouldn't play with me? My father's the kind of guy who likes to win.

"I don't suppose she's had a chance to play a real course yet," Christine said. "This will be a great experience for both of you. If you're as good as your father, Justine, you'll put all the other Kestrels to shame."

I managed a weak smile. Somehow I didn't think that my golf swing was going to put anybody to shame but me. But at least I'd have my dad to myself for the day. And if it went well, maybe we could do it more often.

"What about clubs?" Christine said suddenly. "Justine doesn't have her own set, does she?"

"I've never owned clubs," I said. "Maybe we could go buy a set before Saturday."

"We'll rent from the pro shop on Saturday," my father said firmly. "If it looks like golf is going to be your game, we'll get you your own set then. I'm not springing two hundred dollars for something you're not going to pursue."

This shows how much he had changed since he married Christine. If I had asked him for golf clubs when he visited me at Sagebrush, he would have reached for his checkbook and asked how much. Now he was behaving like anyone else's dad. I wasn't sure I liked it. But I'd give up anything if he was actually going to spend time with me.

The next day when I came home from school, I went straight to my dad's golf closet. I hadn't a clue which club you used for what, and all my father's clubs felt heavy. I thought about going up to the country club for a quick lesson, but then everyone would know that I couldn't play. And I couldn't embarrass my father by making a fool of myself.

I selected a fairly light metal club and took it out to the backyard. I put the ball down on the grass and swung at it. The club came flying, full circle, over my shoulder and hit me in the back. The ball remained where it was on the grass.

I tried again. This time I connected with a satisfying *thwack*. I waited for the ball to land at the other end of the lawn. Instead I was surprised to see it bounce off a stone statue way off to my left and land with a splash in the pool.

I couldn't let anyone see a golf ball in the pool, so I

had to change into my swimsuit and dive down to get it. By that time, Christine had arrived home, so that was the end of golf practice. I really wished that one of my friends would come practice in the park with me, but they couldn't see what I was getting so upset about.

"It's just a social thing, Justine," Ginger had said at lunch that day. "You're not signed up for the pro-am tournament at Pebble Beach."

"I bet most of those wimpy Kestrels can't play worth diddly, anyway," Roni added. "They'll swing, miss, and giggle all day."

"I hope so," I said, biting my lip, "because my dad lives for golf."

"Then maybe it's about time he realizes that his daughter's feelings are more important," Karen said seriously. "Don't worry, Justine. Just go out there and have a good time."

By Saturday morning I was a nervous wreck. My father was really into the tournament, selecting clubs and doing practice swings in the hallway, making Christine yelp each time the club went near one of her Chinese vases.

"Don't worry, honeybun," he said to her. "You're watching a master at work. We're going to show 'em today, aren't we, Justine?"

I nodded, hoping that what we showed them would resemble golf.

My father picked up his golf bag. "See you later, darling," he called to Christine. "We'll be back with a nice big trophy!"

"Bye, Christine. Have a nice day," I called as I followed him to the car. Christine had been very supportive ever since I'd joined the Kestrels. She had even helped me decide what to wear to play golf. I was starting to think this motherhood thing wasn't so bad. At least Christine seemed to be on my side, unlike my friends. All they did was laugh at me, my golf, and the Kestrels.

Several Kestrels were already at the country club when we arrived. They all seemed to have their own golf clubs—a fact that I pointed out to my father.

"If I don't do too well today, don't forget that I only have rented clubs," I said. "They might not be able to find any that are right for me."

"Tell you what," he said, giving me a wink, "if we win the tournament, we'll stop off at the pro shop and you can choose yourself a set. How does that sound?"

"Great," I said, although I knew the only way I was going to win any tournament was if all the other contestants were struck by lightning.

The man in the pro shop picked out a nice set of clubs for me, and Dad and I went down to the veranda to find out our starting time. I noticed that my father was in better shape than many of the other dads. He must have noticed it, too, because he nudged me. "We're the best-looking couple in sight," he whispered in my ear.

We got our starting time and went out to our cart with Chantale and her father.

"This is the life, eh, Craft?" Mr. Franklin said, laughing heartily. "Nothing like spending time with the kids. Greatest investment you can make."

Chantale looked at me and rolled her eyes. I could tell from her face that this was probably the first moment he'd spent with her since birth. I grinned to show that I totally understood.

We drove to the first tee. Mr. Franklin teed off with a perfect swing that landed him on the green. My dad followed, landing slightly closer to the hole. Chantale's swing was also pretty good. I copied their stance, standing feet apart, and gave an impressive swing. Unfortunately the ball wasn't impressed. It was still sitting on the tee.

"Just trying out these clubs," I said, turning to the other three. "They take a little getting used to."

"Take your time, princess," my father said. "No need to rush. Remember, you want a nice smooth follow-through."

I closed my eyes and swung. I heard the *thwack* as my club met the ball, then I heard my dad say, "Not bad. Not bad at all. Now you've got your work cut out for you, Franklin."

I opened my eyes to see my ball lying quite an impressive distance down the fairway. *Great,* I decided. *My problem is solved.* If I just closed my eyes, I'd be fine.

It took me four more strokes to get the ball into the hole, but that was still one better than Chantale. The second hole wasn't so great, but then Chantale hit her ball into the water, so I didn't look like a total dummy.

The third hole was long and difficult. There was a bunker off to one side of the hole, and lots of trees lined the fairway. Chantale's ball went into the bunker. I didn't think I could even hit it that far. I closed my eyes and gave my strongest swing. I heard the horrible sound of my ball hitting a tree, then a *ping* as it struck someone's cart on the path. And then I heard people laughing and clapping.

At least I didn't kill anyone, I thought. Very cautiously I opened my eyes. People had gathered on the green. Mr. Franklin and Chantale were already racing to their cart and speeding forward.

"What is it, Daddy?" I asked. "What did I do?"

He had a big grin on his face. "Well, princess, it looks like you got a hole in one," he said. "Sheer fluke, of course, but it's something I've never managed in all my years of golf!"

People surrounded us as we drove up to the hole. Someone took my picture. "You get the special prize, Justine," Chantale said, looking at me with admiration. "A weekend at the Camelback Resort."

"Wow," was all I could find to say.

After that I didn't play too well, but everyone put my erratic play down to too much excitement. We didn't win the tournament, but my dad didn't care. He was basking in the glory of my hole in one. I went around in a daze with a big smile on my face. It felt great to have my father bragging about me. It even felt great to be told that I was a credit to the Kestrels and they were lucky that I'd joined them. At the reception after the tournament, I received my special award and my dad promised to help me pick out my own set of clubs the next day.

We drove home, talking and laughing.

"We're home, honeybun!" my father yelled in his big voice. "We're starving and I've got a champion golfer here."

He put his arm around me as Christine came out of the living room.

"Go get changed, sweetheart," he said to her. "I'm taking my best girls out to dinner to celebrate."

It was the best moment of my life.

10

When I went to my Kestrels meeting on Monday, everyone greeted me like a returning hero. Even the Kestrels who hadn't taken part in the father-daughter tournament had heard about my hole in one, and they crowded around me, saying nice things.

I'd told Roni, Ginger, and Karen about it, but they hadn't seemed too impressed. In fact, they'd laughed when I described how the ball bounced off a tree and a cart before it reached the green.

"Only Justine could pull a stunt like that," Roni had said.

"You're lucky you didn't kill someone in the process, Justine!" Ginger had added.

But they didn't act like it was any big deal. In fact,

they never said any of the nice things that my new Kestrel friends were always saying. They never told me how clever or interesting I was. Most of the time they told me to shut up when I tried to tell them about my experiences in Europe or at Sagebrush.

Sitting at the Kestrels meeting, I couldn't help wondering if Roni, Ginger, and Karen were the right friends for me after all. My father and Christine hadn't seemed to think so. Now I was beginning to agree. The three of them thought golf tournaments and country clubs were weird. But I liked being part of those things. It was nice to be with girls who appreciated expensive things and thought there was more to life than jeans and shorts. They wouldn't laugh when I said I had no old clothes. They wouldn't tell me to shut up when I said that I'd been skiing in Switzerland.

Chantale's gavel banged on the desk, startling me out of my daze. "First I'd like Serena to give us a report on our very successful golf tournament," she said.

I smiled modestly as Serena talked about my hole in one. They all applauded when they heard I'd won a weekend at the Camelback Resort.

"Now on to more urgent matters," Chantale continued. "Our upcoming dance. Molly, did you get final numbers and talk to the caterer?"

"It's all settled," Molly said. "Although I had to make some pretty desperate calls to come up with the right number of boys."

"I'm sure we'd all like to thank Molly for her hard work," Chantale said. Everyone applauded politely.

"So the caterer is all set?" Chantale asked.

Molly nodded. "There's just one small thing I need to remind you about," she said. "Remember that the caterer only delivers the food. We're responsible for providing our own servers and dishwashers, like we did last year. And as of this moment, we have only two people signed up."

"Only two?" Chantale looked horrified. "How many do we need?"

"Last year we had eight," Molly said.

"Have we advertised around school?" Chantale said, looking annoyed. "Surely there must be eight people who want to make twenty dollars each and don't have anything better to do on a Saturday night."

I raised my hand. "I don't know any of the details about the dance, but I might be able to come up with some people for you."

"That would be great, Justine," Chantale said, smiling sweetly at me. "The dance is Saturday night at the country club ballroom, limited, of course, to Kestrels and their dates. We also invite boys from the local private schools. We find—and I know I'm

117

generalizing—that Alta Mesa boys are . . . well, not the type we want to mix with socially." She wrinkled her cute little nose and gave me a knowing look. I smiled back as she went on. "But we could certainly use anyone you know to help serve and clean up the food."

I blushed again, feeling all the other Kestrels look at me. I didn't want them to think that I was totally pushy. Girls at Sagebrush never liked newcomers who took on too much, too soon. "My friends never do much on Saturday nights. I'm sure they'd like to earn twenty dollars each," I said.

"Terrific. Brilliant," Chantale said, beaming at me as if I'd done something really clever. "How many of them?"

"Three."

"Good. Now we're halfway there."

Then I remembered Danny. He must be pretty hard up, with his dad being a garbage collector and all. Maybe he'd like to make twenty dollars as well. "And I might know somebody else," I said. "I'd have to ask him."

"That's wonderful, Justine. It's a good idea to get some boys because those cases of soda are really heavy. So you'll ask him today and get back to me by tomorrow, okay?"

"Okay," I said.

"I can see that Justine is going to be a really valuable addition, Kestrels," Chantale said. I didn't think that all the faces looking at me completely agreed with her. I'd have to let them know that I was willing to be a team player. So I volunteered to be on the decorating committee for Saturday night. I volunteered to make table settings at home. I even signed up to help shop for the food baskets for the needy. Nobody could say that Justine wasn't willing!

The meeting wasn't over until the end of lunch hour. I knew my friends would have left the tree and would probably be waiting for me by their lockers, so that's where I headed. Chantale and the other Kestrels headed that way, too.

"Justine, move it, girl! We're going to be late!" Roni yelled in her usual loud voice when she saw me come around the corner.

Chantale's nose wrinkled, and I cringed. Why did Roni have to be so loud? "Are those the friends you were talking about?" Chantale muttered.

"Um . . . yeah."

"They're all your friends? Even those creepy guys?"

It was then that I noticed the nerds hanging around my locker, gazing adoringly at my friends.

"Only the girls," I said. "Those boys are always pestering us. They're a big pain."

119

"I've seen them around school. They are totally disgusting," one of Chantale's friends said. "Why don't you tell them to get lost, Justine? You don't actually like them hanging around, do you?"

"I hate it," I said. "And you're right. They *are* disgusting."

"Then be firm, Justine. A Kestrel always speaks her mind," Chantale said. "Tell them to get lost. And for heaven's sake, don't ask anybody like that to serve at our dance. We don't want to be surrounded by creeps."

"Don't worry. I wouldn't dream of it," I said. I left Chantale and walked down the hall to my friends, who were making frantic hurry-up gestures.

"Come on, grab your stuff!" Ginger yelled.

"Walter has invented another new computer program," Karen said. "It tells you what kind of personality you are. We're going to see it demonstrated tomorrow."

"Don't they ever get the message?" I said loudly. "We are not interested in them or their stupid computer programs. I wish they would go back to their swamp and leave us alone."

The nerds looked surprised, then hurt. They shuffled away without saying anything.

"Boy, Justine, you didn't have to be so mean to them," Roni said. "You know they're harmless. It

120

makes them happy to talk to normal girls once in a while."

"They're also very bad for our image," I said. "Do you know that people see us with them and think we're part of their group?"

"Who cares?" Ginger demanded. "People who know us understand that we're just being friendly. It's only people like your frilly-apron friends who care about image."

I glanced over my shoulder, but Chantale and her friends had disappeared.

"So what thrilling event were you planning this week—an overnight trip to Paris? Tennis with Andre Agassi?" Roni asked, grinning at Karen and Ginger.

"Don't ask, she's sworn to secrecy," Karen quipped.

I ignored their sarcasm. "I already told you—the dance on Saturday," I said. "I'm so excited. I get to buy a new prom dress—Christine actually told my dad I needed one. The Kestrels have invited boys from all the best schools, too. Maybe this will be my chance to meet the guy of my dreams—without any help from the Boyfriend Club!"

None of them seemed nearly as excited about the dance as I was. Then I remembered. "Hey, guess what? I even got you guys involved."

"You did?" They looked excited now.

"Sort of. They need people to serve food and clean up, so I volunteered you."

There was a long moment of silence.

"Gee, that was nice of you, Justine," Ginger said finally. "Especially without asking us."

"I-I thought you'd want to do it," I stammered. "I mean, you don't have much to do on Saturday nights, and it pays twenty bucks. . . ."

"Why wouldn't we want to do it?" Karen said, her normally sweet voice sounding cold. "I mean, we don't have any excitement in our lives. It will be a big thrill to watch other girls dancing around and having fun."

"I didn't mean it like that," I said miserably. "I genuinely thought you might enjoy making some easy money. I would have invited you to the dance if I could, but it's for Kestrels only. Maybe you'll be able to meet some of the boys while you're handing around the food."

"We don't need to meet boys," Roni said. "We all have very nice boyfriends of our own who don't expect us to wait on them."

"I'm sorry," I said. "I didn't mean to offend you. I didn't mean it to sound snobby, and now it does. I'll tell Chantale that she'd better find someone else."

I saw a glance pass between Roni and Ginger.

"It's okay, Justine. We'll do it for you," Roni said

with a sigh. "We don't want to let you down the first time you promise to do something for your Kestrels."

"Really? That's so nice of you," I stammered.

Karen touched my arm. "If this is important to you, we'll do what we can to back you up," she said.

"At least it's safer than a visit to the Blackwater Fever club," Ginger said, making us all smile.

"I've been a pain lately," I said. "I'm sorry. I guess I'm just trying to find a niche for myself, like my stepmother says. You all have boyfriends and places to go. I'm just a hanger-on. Maybe I don't want to be a Kestrel forever, but who knows—I could find the guy of my dreams at the dance and we can all live happily ever after."

"And he'll have to be better than Stryker," Karen said. "At least your folks will approve of him."

"That's right," I said. "Maybe my dad will even want to be his buddy!"

The rest of the week passed way too slowly. My friends complained that they never saw me anymore, which was true. The decorations committee met every day, making silk flower centerpieces and place cards for the dance. As I stacked the place cards, I wondered which name I should put next to mine: P. Stuart Atkins III? Rodney Holbrook? Damien Dobrowsky? So many interesting names . . . so many possibilities!

By Wednesday I still hadn't gotten the courage to approach Danny about being a server. Chantale still needed helpers, so I made up my mind to ask him after math.

I didn't even have to wait for Danny after class—he actually called my name. "Hey, Justine. Wait up. I need to talk to you."

Perfect, I thought. I waited for him to catch up to me.

"Listen, Justine, I was wondering," he said, pulling me aside to let other students pass. "The homecoming dance is in a couple of weeks and tickets go on sale this Friday. Would you like to come with me?"

I was shocked. I didn't know what to say. I felt my cheeks getting warm. The homecoming dance—that was big stuff, the first important occasion of the school year. I was sure every Kestrel would be there. And they'd see me with Danny and ask all the wrong questions: Does he belong to our country club? What does his father do? And what if one of them knew him? I could just imagine how I'd feel if one of the Kestrels blurted, "Look, there's Justine with the son of our garbage man!"

"So what do you say, Justine?" Danny said in a soft voice. "It could be fun, right?"

He was looking at me with big, hopeful eyes and I felt like a jerk. Deep down I had a feeling that going to homecoming with Danny *would* be fun. Besides, nobody else had asked me. But it was a risk I couldn't take. Now that I was a Kestrel, I just couldn't be seen with Danny. "Gee, Danny, I wish I could," I said, "but I'm going to be away that weekend . . . with my family."

"Oh," he said. "Too bad." I couldn't tell whether he believed me or not.

"Thanks for asking me," I said.

He gave me a lame smile and started to leave. "Just a minute," I said before he could go, "I've got something to ask you. I wondered if you were free this Saturday night?"

"This Saturday?" The hopeful look came back to his face, but then he shook his head. "No, sorry, I've already got plans," he said. "Not that I'm looking forward to them, but it was something my mother got me into. Parents can be a pain, can't they?"

I smiled and agreed that they sure could.

"Was it something fun?"

"No, not really," I said. "I just needed kids to help out in the kitchen at this dance I'm helping to plan, and I thought you could use the money."

"Are you going to be helping out, too?"

"No. I'm going to be at the dance."

"Oh," he said. "Well, uh, thanks for thinking of me, Justine." The hopeful smile was gone. In its place was—what? Hurt, annoyance, anger? It didn't take a genius to tell that I'd offended him. "See ya around, Justine," he said in a flat voice.

"See ya, Danny," I said, watching him go.

It worked out well, I told myself. *If Danny's upset with me, then at least he won't talk to me so much anymore. He could have been a big embarrassment if the Kestrels had seen him.*

I was about to meet preppy guys from the best schools in Phoenix on Saturday—the kind of guys who were right for me. Danny couldn't compete with that.

So why did I feel so miserable?

11

There were lights twinkling in the potted trees and candles glowing on the tables as I entered the room on Saturday night. I had been there during the day, helping with the decorations, but the end result still caught me by surprise. Pink tablecloths, perfect flower arrangements, lots of candlelight for atmosphere. . . . Those Kestrels sure knew how to do things right. Chantale was standing near the door, dressed in pink silk. I saw her smile at me, but the smile froze on her face.

"Welcome, Justine," she said. "You look . . . uh, very nice."

I immediately saw the reason for her embarrassment. One of the older Kestrels—a tall, elegant senior named Patricia—was standing a few feet away, wearing the same dress as me. I could feel the daggers of Patricia's gaze and the coldness of her friends even before I took two steps into the room. I gave Patricia a weak smile. "Nice dress," I said.

There was no hint of a smile on her face. "A little old for a freshman, though, don't you think? I always feel that girls should look their age."

"Look, I'm sorry, I had no idea," I said, dropping my voice so that only she could hear. "The woman at the boutique told me it was one of a kind."

"That's what she told me, too," Patricia said. "We Kestrels usually check with each other to prevent this sort of embarrassment."

"It's not really an embarrassment," I said, still trying to laugh it off. "After all, it looks pretty good on both of us."

"That's a matter of opinion," she said, and turned back to her friends.

Great going, Justine, I thought. *How to make an enemy in one easy lesson.* Patricia's friends were still giving me hostile glances over their shoulders, and I could imagine what they were saying about me. I slunk into the room and pinned on the corsage that was waiting on a side table with my name on it. It was pink to match the tablecloths and small to show that I was a very new Kestrel. As I fumbled with the pin, I glanced around, trying to see what the selection of guys was like.

There were already quite a few of them there, mostly hanging around the punch bowl, their hands stuck nervously into their pockets. They were all wearing dark suits or blazers and slacks. All of them had the same hairstyle—very short. They were the type of guys my parents would love for me to bring home. And some of them weren't at all bad looking. I began to feel hopeful again. Maybe I actually looked better in the dress than Patricia—maybe that's why she was so mad at me! I grinned to myself.

More people arrived. I made my way around the room until I located my place card, but I didn't recognize any of the names at my table. Obviously I wasn't included with the popular clique. I danced a couple of times with dull guys who stepped on my toes and talked about their plans to go to Harvard. The cute guys seemed to have been snapped up by the seniors. Chantale was dancing wildly. So was Patricia, although the dress looked dangerously tight on her whenever she flung her arms around. I hoped for a loud ripping sound.

At the first available opportunity I went back to the kitchen to see how my friends were doing. As I pushed open the door, there was a great roar of laughter, immediately hushed. Three very red faces looked up at me. My friends were clustered around the sink.

"Oh, Justine, it's only you," Ginger said, letting out a sigh of relief. "We thought it would be that creepy Chantale girl and we'd be caught in the act."

"The act of what?"

Karen glanced at Roni, her mouth twitching in amusement. "Roni was just giving her impression of a snobby Kestrel and she knocked into the table. A whole tray of stuffed eggs slid onto the floor," she said. "We were just wiping them off and putting them back."

"How was I supposed to know that stuffed eggs are slippery?" Roni demanded. Everyone burst out laughing again. "Besides, they won't know the difference. If anyone finds any specks of dust on them, Justine can say they've been rolled in caviar."

"Before I eat anything, are there any other dishes that have had an interesting history?" I asked.

"Not yet, but we haven't tried getting the hot quiches out of the oven yet," Roni said. "That could prove interesting. The pans are really old and disgusting. We have bets on whether the quiches will stick to the gunk on them."

"Roni, that is so gross," Karen said, but they were all still laughing.

"Don't worry, I'll just hold the trays upside down

until the quiches fall onto the floor and then we can pick them up," Ginger teased.

"So what's it like outside, Justine? I haven't had time to take a peek yet," Roni said. "Are you having fun out there?"

I wanted to say that it was boring, but I smiled instead. "Oh, it's a blast," I said. "Those prep school boys actually know how to dance without mashing my toes, and one of them was at the boys' school across the valley from Sagebrush. Isn't that amazing?"

"You seem to be fitting right in. That's great," Karen said softly.

"I want to thank you all for helping me out like this," I said. As I said it I realized it sounded like an Academy Award speech, thanking all the little people. I stopped, confused. I just couldn't seem to talk to these three anymore. "I guess I'd better be getting back or Chantale will come looking for me," I finished lamely.

The room was more crowded than it had been before, and the music had gotten louder and wilder. The floor was a mass of flailing arms and legs. I stood by the door for a while, but nobody asked me to dance. I made my way around to the punch bowl and stood there, wondering why I had ever felt that I belonged with this group of kids. Nobody had bothered to speak to me all evening. Nobody had tried to include me. My card had been placed at a table full of dorks who actually made the nerds look like hunks!

I found myself wishing that I could be having fun with my friends in the kitchen. I even found myself wishing that Danny had agreed to come. *The kitchen would really be rocking if he was there,* I thought. *I bet he'd do a great impersonation of that string-bean dork from Brophy Academy.*

I took a sip of my drink and wondered what was in the punch. I was sure I was seeing things. There, a few feet away from me, was Danny, dressed in a tux and escorting a petite dark-haired girl to the punch bowl. When he saw me, he looked as surprised as I was.

"Justine!" he sputtered. "What are you doing here?"

"I'm a Kestrel."

"Really?" A flash of amusement crossed his face. "I suppose it figures. This was the event you wanted me to work as a busboy for?"

I nodded, still in shock. "I never dreamed, in a million years, that you'd be coming to it as a . . ."

"Well, I have two legs and I own a tux," he said, grinning at my uncomfortable face.

"Yes, but . . ."

"But what?"

"I thought they were only inviting guys from private schools," I said. It was the only polite way I could think

132

of to say that he wasn't really the right type of guy.

He grinned again. "I'm Angie's date," he said. "Angie, have you met Justine yet?"

She looked at me coldly. "I've heard about her," she said. "Hi, Justine."

"Our parents know each other," Danny said. "Our dads are old golf buddies."

"*Your* father plays golf?" I asked, stunned.

"Is that a crime? Guys who own garbage companies are allowed to play golf."

I couldn't speak. His words were just sinking in. Guys who *own* garbage companies. His father owned the company. He didn't drive the truck, he didn't collect the garbage, he wasn't poor. I had never been so mortified in my life. I had been snobby to someone I liked, and now here he was with another girl! He was probably taking her to homecoming, too, since I was too much of a snob to go with him.

I was glad when a few couples pushed between us, heading for the punch bowl. Danny and Angie drifted away, but I was rooted to the ground. I was in shock.

Through my daze, I noticed that the punch was almost gone. Someone went to the kitchen to ask for a refill. Karen emerged a few seconds later, staggering under a big container of punch. None of the guys standing around offered to help her. She held it up and started to pour.

It wasn't her fault that the music chose that second to start up again. Instantly the couple closest to the table launched into a wild, arm-swinging dance. The guy caught Karen's arm just as she was pouring. Purple punch went flying everywhere. It spattered the wall and the pink tablecloth, and some of it got on my dress. But most of it landed on Chantale, standing on the other side of the table. She screamed so loudly that the dancers froze.

"Look what you've done!" she yelled. "You stupid, idiotic, no-brained creep. Look at my dress! It's ruined!"

Karen looked as if she was about to die of embarrassment. "I'm sorry . . . I didn't mean . . ." she stammered.

I waited for someone to come forward and say that it wasn't her fault. I knew that someone should be me. After all, I was Karen's friend. She had only agreed to help out tonight to please me. But Chantale was in hysterics about her dress, shrieking loudly as she ordered her friends to sponge off the purple punch with paper napkins.

"You're going to pay for this!" Chantale screamed.

I opened my mouth, but before I could say anything, Danny stepped forward. "Hey, hold it a minute," he said. "It wasn't her fault. That guy bumped into her and jogged her arm."

Chantale looked from Karen to Danny and back

again. "She should have known better than to pour punch when people were dancing," she said.

"Give her a break; she's only a kid from our school. It's not like you hired professional waiters or something," Danny said. "She was doing her best, and now you're making her feel really bad."

Karen looked like she was about to cry. I knew I should go to her side, put my arm around her, and tell her it was all right. But I didn't get a chance.

"*She's* feeling really bad?" Chantale snapped. "Well, excuse me, but I've just had a three-hundred-dollar dress ruined. How do you think I feel?" Suddenly her gaze fell on my dress and her eyes opened wide in horror.

"Justine!" she gasped. "You've got spots on your lovely new dress, too. You're so nice not to make a fuss about it. Come on, let's get into the bathroom and see if we can wash this off before the stain sets. Help us, Serena, Molly. . . ."

Arms grabbed me and propelled me to the bathroom. I looked back and saw Danny, his arm around Karen's shoulders, taking her back to the kitchen. I felt terrible, but I didn't see how I could break away from the girls who were dragging me off.

There were only a couple of little spots on my dress, and I got the feeling they'd come out easily, but Chantale fussed over me as if it were a major disaster. "Your first Kestrel dance and this has to happen," she said. "I told the rest of the committee that we were being cheap not hiring professional help, but they wanted all the money to go to charity. It's just the way they are. But now this!"

"It's okay, it's really nothing," I said, embarrassed by the amount of attention she was paying to my two tiny spots when she had a purple stain covering half her dress. "I'll be fine. Let's try and do something about you." I picked up a fold of the dress. "Do you think rinsing it would help?"

"I think it's past helping," she said. "I'll have to get a new one. Leave it, Justine, there's no point."

"I'm sorry about your dress," I told her. "It was so pretty, too."

She smiled at me fondly. "These things happen. We just have to be mature and understand that the world is full of creeps. I should get back out there. Come on, Justine, I'll introduce you to some of my friends."

She linked her arm through mine and began chatting cheerfully as we left the bathroom. I suddenly realized what had happened—I was accepted. The accident had made me part of the Kestrel in-crowd, one of the upper-class kids who had a gripe with the creeps serving the food. I was one of Chantale's buddies now. And my friends were the peasants in the kitchen.

I was really confused as Chantale propelled me back into the dance. On the one hand, I was still angry about the way she had talked to Karen. But on the other hand, I was just dying to meet a non-nerd and have the chance to dance with him. What harm could there be in that?

After the dance I'll make it up to Karen, I told myself as I followed Chantale.

12

Chantale swept me across the floor, bravely waving aside sympathetic comments about her ruined dress. When she finally reached her table, she glanced around the group standing nearby for a moment, then grabbed hold of a navy blue sleeve.

"Barry, I've got someone I want you to meet," she said sweetly.

The guy turned around, and I found myself staring into the bluest eyes I'd ever seen. They were bright, summer-sky blue, clear and sparkling. What's more, they were ringed with dark lashes. Quickly I took in the rest of him—straight, angular features, dark wavy hair, navy blue blazer, striped tie . . . the guy was perfect. If Walter could create a boyfriend to order with one of his dumb computer programs, then he would look just like this boy.

"Justine Craft, I'd like you to meet Barry Sanderson," Chantale said in her best hostess voice. "Justine is a new Kestrel, Barry. She's just come from Sagebrush. Isn't that where your cousin goes? Barry is a *senior* at St. Ignatius, Justine."

The blue eyes crinkled at the sides. "Hi," he said. I tried to say hello, but my tongue was stuck to the roof of my mouth. I just smiled instead.

"Would you like to dance?" he asked. Even his voice was gorgeous—smooth and deep, like a radio announcer's. Without waiting for my answer, he slipped an arm around my waist and propelled me onto the floor. It was a slow number, and he held me close.

"So, Justine, do you like your new school?" he murmured. His lips were so close, they tickled my ear.

"I'm beginning to," I said. I could feel a glow coming from his cheek to mine, even though we weren't quite touching.

"Better than Sagebrush, right?" he asked, chuckling. "My cousin Samantha is always complaining about the food and the cold dorms."

"Samantha Ferris? Is she your cousin?"

"Right. A little pain, isn't she? She's always been a whiner."

"We used to call her Wendy Whiner at school," I admitted, laughing.

Barry tightened his grip on me and swung me into a perfect turn. The lights and candles swung around in a blur. I was floating in a haze of happiness. *If this is a dream, then never wake me up,* I thought. I wondered if my friends were watching me from the kitchen. How envious they'd be that I'd snagged the best-looking guy in the room. How much more mature Barry was than Ben or Drew or James. They were just little boys. Barry was almost a man!

The slow dance came to an end. A couple of faster songs followed, leaving us both laughing and gasping.

"Are you about ready to split?" Barry whispered in my ear as he led me back to his table.

"But the dance doesn't end until midnight," I said.

Barry seemed to think I'd said something funny. "A group of us are going over to Chantale's place to party," he said. "You do want to come, don't you?"

"Uh . . . sure. Of course," I stammered. "But I'd better call my dad. He was planning to pick me up here at midnight."

"Tell him I'll run you home," Barry said. "I've got my Beemer outside."

His Beemer, I thought happily. Finally, a boy that my father had to approve of. St. Ignatius, a cousin at Sagebrush, and a BMW, not to mention drop-dead cute! I told Barry I'd meet him outside and ran into the kitchen.

"Hey, you guys! Guess what!" I called. Three angry faces turned to stare at me. Karen's eyes were still red from crying.

"How could you do that, Justine?" Roni demanded. "Chantale yelled at Karen and you didn't even try to stop her."

"I'm really sorry," I said. "I wanted to help, but those girls dragged me into the bathroom. I felt really bad for you, Karen. Honest I did."

"Yeah, sure," Ginger said. "Thank heavens Danny was here. He *really* cares about people."

I swallowed hard. "I'm sorry. I felt terrible, but I didn't know what to do."

"What to do?" Roni repeated. "How about be a good friend? No, you wouldn't know how to do that, I guess. You sure have a lot to learn about friendship, Justine. If you think those kids out there are your friends, then you need your head examined."

"Anyone would have been upset if they'd just had a new dress ruined," I said.

"That's ridiculous," Ginger said.

"That girl Chantale was a total creep," Roni said. "I'd have told her what I thought of her, but Ginger wouldn't let me go out there."

"It wouldn't have helped," Ginger said. "People

like her don't care about people they think are beneath them. If you yelled at her, she would have said you were a bad-mannered peasant."

"Then I would have bopped her one on the nose," Roni said.

"It's okay," Karen said quietly, "I understand that Justine didn't want to take my side with Chantale there. After all, she wants to fit in with her new friends."

This made me feel worse than anything else. "Chantale did act like a jerk, Karen," I said.

"I suppose clothes are important to people like her," Karen said. "And I really did feel bad about spilling the punch. I guess I wrecked your dress, too, Justine."

"It wasn't your fault, Karen. Everyone knows that."

"I just hope she doesn't expect me to buy her a new dress."

"She can afford a new one," I said. "Her family is rolling in dough. Just forget it ever happened, okay?"

"I don't think I'll be able to forget it in a hurry," Karen said. "But you shouldn't be hanging around in here with us. Chantale would be mad if she saw you."

"Yeah, Justine. We don't want to make Chantale mad, do we?" Roni echoed. "You should get back to your *friends* now."

The way she said *friends* made a chill run all the

143

way down my spine. I wanted to say that I was with my real friends already, but the truth was that I didn't deserve to be friends with someone like Karen. I hadn't acted like a friend at all.

"Actually, I came in to call my dad," I said. "He doesn't need to pick me up because Barry is giving me a ride home."

"Barry?"

"Only the most gorgeous guy in the room, and a senior, too. He's going to run me home in his Beemer after the party."

"What party?" Roni asked sharply.

"A group of us are going over to Chantale's house to hang out."

Roni and Ginger exchanged nervous glances. "Do you think your folks will let you leave the dance with kids you don't know?" Roni asked.

"Sure, why not?"

"But they're all way older than you, Justine. You don't know what kind of parties they throw—it could be really wild."

"So? I can handle myself, you know. I've been to bars on the Left Bank in Paris and après-ski parties in Switzerland."

I saw my friends look at one another again.

"But you will tell your dad when you call and get his permission, won't you?" Ginger asked.

"What are you, my chaperon or something?" I demanded. "Or are you just jealous that you haven't been invited to a party by a gorgeous guy?"

"We're really happy for you if you've found a good-looking guy, Justine," Karen said. "We just want to make sure you don't get into a situation you can't handle."

"There's not much I can't handle," I said. "Remind me to tell you about the knife fight I saw in Spain once. Now, excuse me. Barry will be wondering where I am."

I called my father. As I hoped, he and Christine weren't home, so I left a message on the answering machine, telling them that they didn't have to pick me up because I was getting a ride. At least that got me out of answering any embarrassing questions. Then I got my jacket and purse from my table and went looking for Barry.

As I made my way across the dance floor, Danny grabbed my arm.

"Justine, you're not thinking of going to that party, are you?" he demanded.

"I don't see what it's got to do with you," I snapped. Having Danny yell at me was more than I could take. "What is this? Does everybody in this world suddenly think I need a baby sitter?"

"I've heard what their parties are like, that's all," he said.

"Maybe you're another one who's jealous because you're not invited."

"I wouldn't go to a party with those creeps if you paid me," he snapped. "Justine, they're wild and they're a bunch of snobs."

"So maybe I'm a snob, too."

"Yeah," he said, his eyes narrowing. "I didn't want to believe you were, but I guess I was wrong. You turned me down for the homecoming dance because you thought I wasn't good enough for you, didn't you? You were really surprised to see me here tonight. Well, if that's the way you think, then maybe you really *do* belong with them."

"Justine!" Barry called impatiently from the doorway. "We're leaving now."

"Gotta go," I said, pushing past Danny.

"Justine, take care of yourself, okay?" Danny said as I hurried past him.

I ran out to join Barry and a group of kids in the parking lot. The party was over in Paradise Valley, and we got there in about three minutes flat. An Acura filled with a bunch of kids from the dance swung into the street at the same time we did, and we raced the last mile to Chantale's house. For a moment I was caught up in the excitement and the incredible feeling of speed and power. Then we reached a stop sign just as another car was crossing the intersection. Our two cars shot past, one on either side of him, as he jammed on his brakes and blasted his horn at us.

"What a jerk." Barry laughed. "Guys who own Buicks shouldn't be allowed out at night."

I laughed, too, because he seemed to expect it. But inside I was feeling sick and scared. Had we really missed death by inches or was I over-reacting?

Inside Chantale's spacious home, the party was already in full swing. Kids were standing around the pool, drinking beer and dancing to the loud throb of music.

"Here," someone said, and put a can of beer into my hand.

I opened my mouth to say that I didn't drink beer, but then I closed it again. These kids would think I was a dweeb if I refused to drink. I opened the beer and pretended to take little sips. Barry didn't hesitate. He chugged his whole can down. "That's better," he said. "Come on, let's go find somewhere we can be alone."

Out of the corner of my eye I spotted one couple, already getting really friendly on a garden chaise. I turned away, embarrassed. I hoped Barry didn't have ideas like that, but I was pretty sure that was exactly what he had in mind. He'd think I was a baby if I tried saying no to him. But what else could I do? I'd never even kissed a guy before!

I pictured Danny's worried face, and my friends' worried faces. *They knew what I was getting into here,* I thought. *They really cared about me. They didn't want me to come. . . .* If only it hadn't mattered so much to me to feel that I belonged with the Kestrels.

The music ended, followed by silence.

"Have you finished your beer yet?" Barry asked. "Come on, drink up."

"I don't really like beer," I said lamely.

"Why didn't you say so?" he said. "There's wine coolers in the fridge."

He took my hand and led me in that direction. I stood there, not knowing what to say or do next, while he pulled a wine cooler out of the refrigerator.

As it happened, I didn't have to think about what to do next. A big voice boomed behind me, "Justine? What do you think you're doing?"

My father's face was almost purple as he glared first at me, then at the wine cooler in my hand. I didn't care how mad he was—I had never been so happy to see anyone in my life.

"I didn't believe it when your friends called and told me what you were up to," he said.

"My friends called you?" I stammered. "My

friends actually called you and snitched on me?"

"And lucky for you that they did," he said. "You know you're not allowed to drink. You know you don't belong at a party like this. Look at these people. Half of them are already drunk!"

"But these are the Kestrels, Daddy," I said, a note of delight creeping into my voice. "These are the people you wanted me to hang out with."

"I had no idea," he said angrily. "I thought that guy Franklin would know how to raise a child decently. He's always boasting about all the interest he took in his kids. . . . If this is how his daughter has turned out, then you'd do well to stay away from her."

He grabbed my arm. "Come on, get your things. We're going home."

13

I sat there, shivering slightly in the chill of the night, listening to the purr of my father's Mercedes and trying to think of something to say. *Now he really must be mad at me,* I thought. *Now I really will get sent back to Sagebrush.* And I couldn't think of a thing to say that would possibly make it better.

At last I couldn't stand the silence any longer. "Daddy," I said, "I want you to know that I wasn't drinking. I was letting Barry give me a wine cooler, but I wasn't going to drink it. I didn't touch the beer they gave me—"

He gave a tired sigh. "It's okay, Justine," he said. "I know you're not stupid enough to drink. I guess it's all my fault. I wanted to get you into that crowd at school. I thought you needed to meet the right sort of kids. Boy, was I wrong!"

"They weren't the kind of kids I really wanted to hang out with," I said. "They were exactly like the kids at Sagebrush—snobby and spoiled and mean. Chantale humiliated my friend Karen, just because she spilled punch by accident." I took a deep breath. "I didn't even say anything, Dad. I should have spoken up and defended Karen. I feel really bad."

"You should always speak up when you see something wrong, Justine," he said. "Too many bad things happen in this world because people are afraid to speak up. And you should always stick by your friends . . . especially good friends like yours."

"I thought you didn't like my friends," I said in amazement. "You said they were outsiders, and I needed to be with kids who were in the middle of things."

"Maybe I have some learning to do, too," he said. "Those friends of yours are pretty gutsy, Justine. Roni told me that I had to get over to Chantale's, and fast. She said she was scared that you were getting into a situation you couldn't handle. That shows maturity, Justine. I like that. You stick with those girls and you won't go wrong."

"I only hope I haven't blown it with them already," I said miserably. "I haven't been a very good friend lately. I guess I've never had a chance to learn how to be a true friend before. You always moved me around so much. . . ."

"I know," he said softly. "I haven't been the greatest father to you. That's why I want so much for us to be a family now. With the new baby coming, we have a chance for a real family life. I can make up for all the years I never really got to know you . . . if only you'd give us a chance, Justine. Especially Christine. She really cares about you."

"You could have fooled me," I said. "All she ever does is complain about how I mess up the house. When I came back from that rock club, I was scared and hurt, and all she could say was that I didn't look good."

"She was really upset," my father said. "She blamed herself. She kept saying, 'If only I knew how to reach her, maybe she'd have turned to me instead of running off.' She really wants this family to work, Justine. Please give her a chance. For me?"

"I guess," I said shakily. I wasn't used to heart-to-heart talks with my father. It made me feel like crying.

Christine opened the front door the instant we pulled into the driveway. "Did you find her?" she called. "Oh, thank goodness. She's okay."

She came running down the steps toward us.

"You should have seen the party going on at

153

Franklin's house," my father said as he climbed out of the car. "Talk about out of control. I'm sure someone's called the cops by now. I never thought Franklin would let his kid run wild like that."

"Well, you can't blame Justine," Christine said. "We were the ones who forced her into that group. She was probably just going along because everyone else did." She took my arm. "Come on, sweetie. You've had enough excitement for one night. Go on up to bed and I'll bring you a hot chocolate."

She came up just as I finished undressing and helped me into bed. "It's funny," she said, perching on the bed beside me. "We go to college and learn all sorts of complicated facts and figures, but nobody ever teaches us how to be parents. I don't know how to get through to you, Justine. All these things you've been doing—that rock club and now this party—they're just ways to get back at your dad and me, aren't they?"

I thought about this and nodded slowly. "I suppose I did want to get back at you. I wanted my dad to notice me for a change. And I wanted to pay him back for marrying you."

"Do you hate me so much?" she asked.

I looked down and said nothing.

"I've really tried, but I don't know how to make you stop seeing me as the enemy," she said at last. "I do care about you, you know."

154

I looked up into her face. There were tears in her eyes.

"I didn't think you cared," I said. "I didn't think you wanted me around. Especially now with the baby coming."

"What a terrible thing to say. Of course I want you around. It was my idea to bring you home from boarding school so that we could be a real family. If I hadn't wanted you around, I could have left you there."

I digested the truth of this. "You're always complaining about me," I said at last.

"I'm just trying to do what any good mother would do, Justine. You've been used to getting your own way all the time, doing what you want whenever you want. You've lived for years without a mother, and I think maybe you need someone to be there for you. I might not be too great at mothering, but I'm trying. I admit I've been a little heavy-handed sometimes, but you haven't given me a chance, either. You've been determined to hate me, no matter what I do."

I looked down at my satin quilt, embarrassed that this was true. "I was jealous of you," I admitted. "It's always been my dad and me until now."

"Your dad popping in for two minutes before he sent you off to another boarding school? Is that better than what you've got now?"

"I guess not," I whispered.

She reached out and squeezed my hand. "Then let's try to make a go of this," she said. "I'm going to need all the help and support I can get. I know nothing about having babies, and frankly, I'm a little scared. I'm going to need you, Justine."

"Okay."

"Then let's start over, all right? I think we could be good friends. We could go shopping together, and I need someone to help me plan a nursery—your father's hopeless. You know him, he just says 'Whatever you want is fine with me' and hands you his credit card."

"That's Dad!" I said.

"Maybe we can educate him, now that he has two women in the house," she said, giving me a knowing smile. "We'll shape him up yet. We'll have him changing diapers and cooking us dinner!"

I smiled back. "Yeah!"

"Friends?" she asked.

"Friends."

She hugged me tightly. Slowly my own arms came around her, and I hugged her back. Then she tucked me in, just the way a mother would do. It felt pretty good.

Early next morning I had my dad drive me over to Ginger's house, where I knew my friends had spent the night. It was the first time that the three of them had had a sleepover without me, and I felt kind of shy as I rang the doorbell.

Ginger came to the door in her pajamas. "Justine!" she exclaimed. "You're the last person I expected to see. Come on in, we're just having pancakes. Roni was trying to flip one and it stuck to the ceiling."

I followed her into the kitchen. I could hear Roni and Karen laughing.

"Hi, guys," I said quietly.

The laughter faded. "Hi, Justine," Karen answered.

"I had to come over right away to tell you how sorry I was about last night," I said. "And to thank you for calling my dad and sending him off to rescue me."

The three of them exchanged looks. "We thought you'd be mad at us," Karen said.

"I was too happy to see my father to be mad," I said, "and I realized that you guys really care about me. You were right—that party was a situation I couldn't handle. That guy was a jerk, and everyone was drinking and being wild. I was terrified."

"Well, it's really Danny you should thank for saving you," Karen said. "He knew what those parties were like. He told us that if we didn't call your dad, he would."

"Really? And I was so rude to him," I said, my cheeks flushing bright red at the memory. "He invited me to the homecoming dance and I turned him down."

"You got invited to the homecoming dance and you said no?" Ginger shrieked. "Justine, how could you?"

"Do you think it's too late to tell him I'm free after all?"

"You could try," Karen said. "Maybe he'll understand that being with the Kestrels went to your head for a while."

"It sure did," I said. "I thought that I'd found my niche, as my father calls it. But the only thing that belongs in a niche with the Kestrels is a cockroach. Those girls are so rude—they're just like the girls at Sagebrush. I hated it there!"

Three surprised faces looked at me. "You hated it at Sagebrush?" Roni asked. "But you're always talking about how superior Sagebrush is compared to Alta Mesa."

"I know," I said. "I say stupid things when I'm insecure. Sagebrush did have skiing and ballet and all that fancy stuff, but the girls were all like Chantale Franklin. They could be really sweet if you were in their clique, but they were totally horrible if you weren't. I wasn't in anyone's clique. In fact, I never had good friends until I met you guys. I can't believe I was dumb enough to wreck my friendship with you."

"It's okay, Justine," Karen said. "You were also

smart enough to see through the Kestrels before it was too late."

"So you'll still be my friends?" I asked excitedly. "You're willing to forgive and forget?"

"We're big enough to do that. Right, guys?" Roni said.

"I'll do anything to make it up to you," I told them.

"Well, there is one thing you can do . . ." Roni began.

"What?"

"Get that pancake down from the ceiling."

I wasn't sure how I was going to face the Kestrels in school on Monday. Would Chantale be mad at me for leaving her party in such a hurry? What would she say when she heard I wasn't coming to any more business meetings to plan the next extravaganza?

At lunchtime I told my friends that I was going to officially resign from the Kestrels. I had just started down the hall in the direction of the meeting room when I heard Chantale's voice up ahead. I turned the corner and saw a group of Kestrels bearing down on Danny.

"Hey, you," Chantale called to him.

He turned around and stopped. "You want to talk to me?"

"I sure do," Chantale said coldly. "I don't know who you think you are, but you were at our dance on

Saturday night and you were rude to me in front of my guests."

"I was rude to you?" Danny sounded amazed. "I think it was the other way around. You were incredibly rude to one of the people who had kindly volunteered to help out."

"Kindly volunteered?" Chantale snorted. "They were getting paid twenty bucks. They should have been grateful."

"You people think your money can buy anything," Danny said. "You make me sick."

"I want you to know that you will not be welcome at any of our functions in the future. You obviously don't fit in with the Kestrels."

Danny was grinning. "You're darned right I don't," he said. "I only went to your stupid dance as a favor to my father's golf buddy."

"Your father's golf buddy?" Chantale repeated, suddenly looking uncomfortable.

"Yeah, Angelo Demartini. You know, the president of the country club? But don't worry. Nothing in the world would ever make me attend another of your snobby, boring dances. You might have money, Chantale, but you sure don't have class."

"How dare you!" Chantale yelled. "Just get out of my sight, or you'll be sorry!"

One of her followers grabbed her arm. "Don't

upset yourself, Chantale. He's not worth it. Come on, we'll be late for the Kestrels meeting."

They turned in my direction. "Justine!" Chantale cooed as soon as she saw me. "There you are! We didn't know what happened to you at the party—you just disappeared. Barry was so sad you had to leave. Did you get the spots out of your dress?" She came over and took my arm as though we were best friends. "Come on, we're already late for our meeting, thanks to that creep."

I could see Danny lingering at the far end of the hall. "I'm not coming to the meeting," I said.

There was absolute silence in the hall.

"Aren't you feeling well?" Chantale asked sweetly.

"I've never felt better, thanks," I said. "I've just realized that I have no desire to be a Kestrel or spread my wings or look down on the world, thank you. Find someone else to make your silk flowers and your place cards. I quit."

"You can't quit!" Her voice was trembling. "You took the oath."

"That was before I realized that you were a bunch of stuck-up snobs," I said. "Now, excuse me, but I have to apologize to someone."

I pushed past them and ran down the hall to Danny. He was looking at me with big, solemn eyes. "You really quit the Kestrels?"

"I really did."

161

"That took guts. Chantale is not the kind of person you'd want as an enemy."

"Better than having her for a friend," I said.

We looked at each other and smiled. "I'm sorry I was a jerk," I said. "Thank you for looking out for me. You were right. It wasn't my kind of party."

"That's okay," he said, looking a little embarrassed. "Forget about it."

"Um, you know, Danny, my family isn't going away on homecoming weekend anymore. I just wondered if you'd asked anybody else to the dance yet?"

"Not yet," he said.

"Then I was sort of wondering if the invitation was still on?"

He looked at me, long and hard. I'd never noticed how dark and deep his eyes were before—how they sort of glowed with inner lights. "There's only one thing, Justine," he said solemnly.

"What?"

"If you come with me to homecoming, we'll have to ride there in my dad's garbage truck."

"Shut up," I said, hitting him on the arm. "Your dad plays golf with the president of the country club. Besides, arriving in a garbage truck would cause quite a sensation!"

He took my hand. "In that case, lady, you've got yourself a date!"

162

About the Author

Janet Quin-Harkin has written over fifty books for teenagers, including the best-seller *Ten-Boy Summer.* She is the author of the *Friends* series, the *Heartbreak Café* series, and the *Senior Year* series. She has also written several romances.

Ms. Quin-Harkin lives with her husband in San Rafael, California. She has four children. In addition to writing books, she teaches creative writing at a nearby college.

**Here's a sneak preview of
The Boyfriend Club™ #5:**

Ginger's New Crush

My heart hammered inside my chest. Beside me, Scott was barely breathing. The survival of Spirit Rock depended on what we found in this burial site.

Dr. Delgado opened the basket cautiously. "This is the grave of a person of importance," he said. "A great medicine man, I would guess." He got to his feet. "If the pattern is true to other burial sites of the ancient Pima, then I think we'll find several such graves up here."

"Does that mean that Spirit Rock really is an important Indian site?" Scott asked.

"Undoubtedly," Dr. Delgado said.

"And they won't be able to build their resort on it?" Scott insisted.

"I think that public opinion would be against destroying such a historical treasure," Dr. Delgado said. "I am going to take steps immediately to see that this hill is declared a historic monument of the Pima tribe."

"We've done it, Ginger!" Scott yelled excitedly. "You've done it! You were the one who found it! You're a genius! I love you!" He picked me up and swung me around in his strong arms. Sky and rock flashed past me, and all I could see was Scott's face, his blue eyes smiling down into mine. Had he really said "I love you?" *Could this be happening to me?* I wondered.

The rest of the morning passed in a daze. I might have been up on Spirit Rock for one hour or one day or one lifetime. All I could see was Scott's eyes laughing down into mine. I could feel his warm breath on my cheek and hear those words over and over, "I love you."

If this was one of my daydreams, I never wanted it to stop. I knew that this had gone beyond wanting to make Ben jealous. I didn't care if Ben ever came back from his football tournament. I was hopelessly, deeply, completely, and utterly in love with Scott Masters!

By the afternoon, things got pretty chaotic. Someone had gone down to send a message back to the museum and they must have alerted the media, because suddenly we were surrounded by cameras and microphones.

166

"I understand you're the young lady who made this important discovery," a dark-haired reporter asked. I recognized her from evening TV. She asked me a bunch of questions and then told me that they were planning to do a feature segment on "Kids Who Make a Difference," starring Scott and me. She asked if we could come down to the studio later in the day to tape interviews and put the piece together. I said I might have time to squeeze it into my busy schedule!

"You see, Ginger. Instant stardom," Scott teased. "I bet you never thought saving Spirit Rock would end up like this."

"Never in a million years," I agreed. Would my friends ever believe that I had saved Spirit Rock, become a celebrity, and made Scott Masters fall in love with me all in the same day? I found it hard to believe myself.

I don't even remember coming down the mountain. I think I floated all the way. My feet didn't touch the rocky path once. Scott was there, so close that I brushed against him as we went through the narrow parts. I longed for him to take my hand, but I guess he felt that wouldn't be right. I mean, real archeologists don't go around holding hands on the job, do they? But it was enough just to have him there beside me. When he spoke to me, his eyes positively glowed. My face was glowing, too. I must have looked like one huge grin as more and more people said nice things to me.

At the bottom I stopped to pull up a couple of the stakes. "They won't be needing these anymore," I said. "I think I'll use them to start the barbecue."

Everyone applauded. I felt as if there was nothing in the world I couldn't do.

"Do you want a ride to the studio?" Scott asked.

"I'd like to go home and freshen up first," I said. "I want to look good for my one TV appearance in life."

"I think you look fine," he said.

"Maybe I should just comb my hair and put on some makeup," I suggested. "And change my shorts. These have dirt all over them."

"Okay," he said. "I'll drive you home and wait for you."

As we drove up, I saw that Ben's truck was already in the driveway. I couldn't believe my luck. *Now he'll see what happens when a guy ignores Ginger Hartman,* I told myself. This was my great moment of triumph, the moment that made up for the hurt I'd felt when I overheard that conversation in the locker room.

"I'll be right back," I called to Scott, jumping down from the Jeep. I flung open the front door and made my grand entrance. Todd and Ben weren't sitting on the living room sofa, for once, which was kind of disappointing.

168

"Todd? Anybody home?" I yelled.

Instantly Todd appeared from his room. "Oh, you're back, finally," he said. "Ben's been driving me crazy, waiting for you to come home."

"I'm not stopping," I said. "I have to change quickly and get out of here—"

"You can't go out now," Todd said. "Ben has the most amazing news!"

"I have the most amazing news myself," I said.

"But wait until you hear Ben's news," Todd cut in. "Ben, get out here and tell her!"

Ben appeared from Todd's bedroom. "Hi, Ginger," he said. His face was glowing, just like Scott's. "Guess what? They put me in at wide receiver."

"And tell her the rest," Todd went on. He turned to me. "He scored the winning touchdown! He was amazing. He caught the pass, broke about five tackles, and went all the way—and we won the tournament!"

"Congratulations," I said, "but wait until you hear *my* news. I have just single-handedly saved Spirit Rock, and I'm going to be interviewed for a Channel Ten feature."

I waited for them to be impressed. Nothing happened. Disgusted, I started to push past them into my bedroom.

"When will you be back?" Ben asked.

"The guys are throwing a party in Ben's honor," Todd said. "You have to come."

I looked from my brother to Ben. "I have to come?" I repeated.

"Yeah . . . the guys will expect Ben to bring a date," Todd went on, since Ben seemed reluctant to talk.

I could feel the anger boiling up inside me. "You expect me not to be interviewed by a TV station so that Ben can take me to a party? Is that what I'm hearing?"

"Of course not," Ben said hastily. "Go do your TV thing first. I'm sure it won't take more than a couple of minutes."

"Of course," I said, giving him my sweetest smile. "Why should anything I've done be worth more than a couple of minutes on TV? I mean, it's not like it's a winning touchdown or anything."

"Right," Todd agreed. He really is dumb sometimes.

"You guys make me sick," I snapped. "Last week you sneaked around behind my back so you could go to a party with a bunch of dumb cheerleaders, and now suddenly you've decided that you want me around again because Mr. Studly Wide Receiver needs a girl gazing at him adoringly to boost his image. Well, thanks, but no thanks. I'm not a book you can take off the shelf when it's convenient for you and put back when it's not. I'm a person with feelings. And you know what?" I paused dramatically. "I don't even need you anymore, Ben Campbell. I have Scott waiting for me outside. That's *Scott,* as in Scott Masters—you know, the famous senior? He wouldn't sneak around behind my back to spend an evening with a bunch of cheerleaders."

I rushed into my room and shut the door in their astonished faces. Rapidly I threw everything I owned out of my drawers until I came up with a pair of shorts that didn't look wrinkled and my pale blue halter top. A little mascara, a healthy amount of blush . . . no time for a curling iron, but I caught up my ponytail with my best velvet scrunchie. A quick squirt of G iorgio that Roni had given me last Christmas, and I was ready.

I ran out again, past two dazed-looking guys. Apparently they didn't know what to do when a girl fought back and wanted her own way. Well, they should be used to this girl by now. I'd never taken any nonsense from either of them, and I wasn't about to start.

Ben got up and followed me to the front door. "Ginger, wait," he said. "I didn't mean to upset you. . . ."

I turned back to him. "Not last week? Not when I overheard you in the locker room saying that I meant nothing to you? That I was just a little kid? Well, Scott doesn't seem to think I'm a little kid. He thinks I'm pretty special."

I opened the front door. "Good-bye, Ben. Enjoy your party. Maybe you can find one of those dippy cheerleaders to go with you."

"He might just do that!" Todd yelled after me. But Ben didn't say anything as I ran out to the waiting Jeep.

You don't need
—— a boyfriend to join! ——

Now you and your friends can join the real Boyfriend Club and receive a special Boyfriend Club kit filled with lots of great stuff only available to Boyfriend Club members.

- **A mini phone book for your special friends' phone numbers**
- **A cool Boyfriend Club pen**
- **A really neat pocket-sized mirror and carrying case**
- **A terrific change purse/keychain**
- **A super doorknob hanger for your bedroom door**
- **The exclusive Boyfriend Club Newsletter**
- **A special Boyfriend Club ID card**

All this for just $3.50!

If you join today, you'll receive your special package and be an official member in 4-6 weeks. Just fill in the coupon below and mail to: The Boyfriend Club, Dept. B, Troll Associates, 100 Corporate Drive, Mahwah, NJ 07430

❏ **Yes**, I want to be a member of the real Boyfriend Club. I have enclosed a check or money order for $3.50 payable to The Boyfriend Club.

Name_____

Address_____

City_____State_____Zip_____

Age_____Where did you buy this book?_____

Sorry, this offer is only available in the U.S.

ADVICE EXCHANGE

Boyfriend Club Central asked:

What can you do to meet new friends when you're the new kid in school?

And you said:

Go to after-school sporting events.

- Debra M.,
Los Angeles, CA

Try out for the school play.

- Geri K.,
Coopersburg, PA

Invite some kids in your class to go to your house after school.

- Mary P., Wichita, KS

Introduce your-
self to someone
who looks friend-
ly. Ask them to
introduce you to
their friends.
- Susan P., Newark, NJ

Run for student
government.
- Debbie D., Setauket, NY

Join a sports
team.
- Jill O.,
Sweetwater, TX

Ask someone where
everyone hangs out on
the weekends. Maybe
they'll invite you.
- Diana N., Reston, VA

Now we want to know:
What can you do to cheer up a friend when she's having boy trouble?

Write and tell us what you think, and you may see
your advice in a future ADVICE EXCHANGE:

Boyfriend Club Central
Dept. B
Troll Associates
100 Corporate Drive
Mahwah, NJ 07430